Scorched Souls
Royal Bastards MC
Atlantic City Chapter
Book 2

Written By: Kris Anne Dean
Edited By: Sarah DeLong, DeLong Words
Editor
Elise Gedicke
Cover Design By: Crimson Syn- Syn Ink
Books LLC

ROYAL BASTARDS MC SERIES
SIXTH RUN

Kristine Dugger : Crazy Psycho
KL Ramsey : Lost in Yonkers
Barbara Nolan: Loving Smoke
Crimson Syn: Tormented by Regret
Elizabeth N. Harris: Warden
Liberty Parker : Butcher's Destruction
Morgan Jane Mitchell : Hard Knox
B.B. Blaque: Royal Family
Darlene Tallman : Kraken's Release
H.J. Marshall: Roughstock
Claire Shaw : Tyres
Kathleen Kelly : Highway
J. Lynn Lombard : Jaded Red
India R. Adams : Praying for Fire
Nikki Landis : Grim's Justice
Dani René : REV
Verlene Landon : Snagged by Hook
Kris Anne Dean : Scorched Souls
J.L. Leslie : Worth it All
Jena Doyle: Blood and Whiskey
K.D. Latronico: Wherever I May Roam
Sapphire Knight : Toxic Biker
Nicole James : Taking What's Ours
Rae B. Lake: Sins and Paradise
Kristine Allen: Blade
Roux Cantrell: Hell Bent
Daphne Loveling : Deadly North

M Merin : Big Timber
Amy Davies: Seized by Solo
J.A. CollardAuthor : In Too Deep
Elle Boon : Royally Embraced
Murphy Wallace : Misery and Ecstasy
Theta James: Demon in the Shadows
Chelle C. Craze & Eli Abbott

Royal Bastards MC Facebook Group -
https://www.facebook.com/groups/royalbasta
rdsmc/
Website- https://www.royalbastardsmc.com

ROYAL BASTARDS CODE

PROTECT: The club and your brothers come before anything else and must be protected at all costs. **CLUB** is **FAMILY**.

RESPECT: Earn it & Give it. Respect club law. Respect the patch. Respect your brothers. Disrespect a member and there will be hell to pay.

HONOR: Being patched in is an honor, not a right. Your colors are sacred, not to be left alone, and **NEVER** let them touch the ground.

OL' LADIES: Never disrespect a member's or brother's Ol 'Lady. **PERIOD.**

CHURCH is MANDATORY.

LOYALTY: Takes precedence over all, including well-being.

HONESTY: Never **LIE, CHEAT,** or **STEAL** from another member or the club.

TERRITORY: You are to respect your brother's property and follow their Chapter's club rules.

TRUST: Years to earn it...seconds to lose it.

NEVER RIDE OFF: Brothers do not abandon their family.

Warning:

Welcome to the Atlantic City, NJ chapter of the Royal Bastards. Our world features a one-percent motorcycle club that isn't suitable for fragile hearts. If you're ready to unleash your inner badass read on. You can expect bad boys, dangerous liaisons, forbidden love, steamy scenes, violence and sexual triggers. If you're on the fence this book may not be for you.

Reader discretion is advised, but swooning is highly encouraged.

If you're still here...
Tread carefully... you have been warned...
Let the seductive chaos begin!

Backdraft

Burning embers follow me wherever I go. The flames dance in my dreams, calling to me, daring me to walk with them. Their Siren's song taunts me, even while I rest. There is no escape from the heat licking my skin, the inferno blazing through my body.

When an angel wearing a halo of fire emerges from the flames, I have to have her. Her touch ignites an inferno inside me that's certain to leave us both a smoldering pile of ash.

Zoey

My savior is dark, brooding and dangerous. He took me and stole my heart, igniting a passion like I've never known. My innocence is no match for a man that looks like sin.

His flesh marred with tattoos, burns and scars don't scare me. They calm the infatuation crawling deep below my skin.

I'm drawn to him in ways I've never felt before. The way his eyes dance with fire before burning me to my core. The way his hands caress my aching skin.

He tells me I'm his angel, but one touch could send us both to hell.

Chapter 1
Backdraft

My head is pounding like a jackhammer when I come to hogtied on a slab of concrete. Slivers of light streak the floor in front of me, scattering around the fragments of dust floating in the air. I follow the glare up to their source and find myself enclosed in a small space made from old, worn boards. The pungent smell of musty, rotting wood mixes with the stench of sweat from the suffocating heat pressing down on my sore body. Shifting my weight into an upright position, I pry my arms apart with all my strength. The tape around my wrists snaps, letting me quickly undo the binds around my ankles. When I draw my hand to the back of my head, I find the reason for the pain. There's a knot the size of my fist, hurting like a motherfucker under my touch. The blood sticks to my fingers as I slowly recall what happened.

I tracked my target down to a secluded area deep in the steep hills outside Nashville, Tennessee. I spent days searching for a way into the guarded compound surrounded by thick growth of oak, hickory, and maple. Circling the surrounding terrain and formulating a plan to penetrate the point hiding deep within the wooded area. The compound was surrounded by jagged rocks and thick brush, damn near impenetrable from any point but the main road leading in. I was ready to run through the gate, guns blazing, when an opportunity I had to take presented itself. The convoy of trucks slowly climbing the narrow gravel road to the top provided the perfect cover. Ducking out of the brush, I hoisted myself onto the tailgate of the rear truck and slipped into the back.

The bumps and dips in the rocky terrain are the perfect distraction for my added weight until the convoy rolls to a stop. Laying still, I wait while the driver exchanges words with another man on foot. Boots grinding heavily on the gravel sends warning flares off in my gut. With adrenaline coursing through my veins, I spring into action. Digging into the concealed pocket of the tactical vest strapped beneath my cut, my fingers close around a small bottle cap. Swiftly, I rip open a pack of cigarettes, extracting a lump of malleable clay. I mold it expertly around the head of a match and a remote charge, ensuring its secure placement within the cap. My heart pounds in my chest as I survey the interior of the truck's cargo bed, searching for a prime location to plant it. I pinpoint the perfect spot, nestled snugly within a groove along the top ledge. As I tap the cap against my knuckles, a surge of anticipation courses through me. What it lacks in size and devastation, it makes up for in shock and awe. With quick fingers, I affix the cap bomb. Despite my training and knowledge, the most challenging part lies in waiting for the opportune moment to unleash my calculated assault. Every second feels like an eternity, poised on the brink of chaos, awaiting the perfect moment to detonate my calling card.

As the footsteps grow closer, I roll out of the back and dive for cover while they make their way down the line searching the trucks. Once again, I find myself up to my neck in overgrown weeds. I'm so sick of the fucking woods. I grew up in a small town where all I ever found was boredom and trouble. We didn't have trees with trunks as thick as I am like they do out here. My mind drifts back to a fire I set to some rotted trees, doused in kerosene, that needed to be cut down. The breeze picked that shit up and snowed burning ash downwind for days. What can I say, growing up in the middle of nowhere the only thing for teenagers to do is drink, fuck, and set shit on fire. It took moving to the city before I came into my own and developed the skill set that earned me the road name, Backdraft.

Swatting at the gnats and mosquitoes, my foot catches on something sharp. Flaying my arms outward to catch my balance only serves as a propeller as I careen into the dirt. The shrill wail of an air horn has me scrambling to my feet and taking cover behind a tree while I search out the source of the alarm. The foliage is thick and the best I can tell is it's somewhere overhead. The snap and crackle of twigs and branches means I have company. Even with a silencer on my Glock 19, bullets will only draw more unwanted attention, so I click the safety in place and tuck my gun into the holster under my cut. This fight will have to be handled silently.

I'm skilled in many things, fighting is just one of them. When you grow up like I did, you learn how to defend yourself first and how to fight second. While other boys my age were hitting dingers on the baseball field or running the ball, I was mastering both and those skills are about to become invaluable. I move through the maze of trees and weeds as quietly as a man of my size can. The best way to win a fight is to never let them see you coming. Staying in the shadows of overgrown brush, I move toward the footsteps. Positioning myself just out of sight but very much in earshot, I draw out a long, low whistle. The man stills in his tracks, his back taut as he scans for the source he'll never find. From behind him, a branch rustles through the leaves, after leaving my hand in a stealthy javelin throw. He jerks around, drawing his gun higher. While his back is turned, I reposition myself behind another large tree a few feet over and repeat the process. His head snaps around as I draw out another long whistle, now an octave higher. Followed by the frantic snap of his neck as he spins towards the rock that lands behind him with a heavy thud. Shifting to the right, I use my advantage to haul myself towards him. As he twists back around, I reach out and grab him by the throat. Twisting my arm, I force him to the ground while he gasps for breath. Before I can reach into my pocket for my blade, a sharp sting rips through my head and everything goes dark.

I'm still processing my predicament when a subtle beep disrupts the silence, followed by the distant tick of a clock.

Fuck.

I've done enough research on this group to know exactly what I'm dealing with even before I make it to my feet and locate the bomb. The ticking rapidly increases as the timer counts down. Stalking toward the door, I grip my hand around the handle and push. The resistance confirms my suspicions, I'm locked inside. With a fucking bomb.

Son of a bitch.

I'm way over my head here. I'm an expert on how to stoke a fire or starve a flame, hell I can make pipe bombs and gasoline traps with my eyes closed but this is on a whole different level. I study the contraption of metal and wires, scratching my head. This is unlike any nine-one-one drama on television. I have no idea what wire to pull but I know who might. Thank fuck the stupid pricks left me with my phone and my weapons. I can only assume they figured either the bomb would tear me limb from limb or if I broke free, I'd blow my brains out first.

There are only seven numbers in my contacts with the first being my President. Hitting call on my cell phone, I switch it to the speaker and sit it down. While waiting for an answer, I search my surroundings from top to fucking bottom.

"Pres, I'm in fucking trouble here. In ten minutes, I'm a dead man unless someone knows how to get me out of this shit."

"Talk about balls to the wall, brother. Hang tight," Aero's voice is faint, but I make out the sound of him calling in the troops. There are muffled voices and shuffling coming through the line.

I haven't taken my eyes off the timer since I realized there's not a quick exit. With my bare hands the only tools at my disposal, it would take too long to peel the weathered boards off the rusty nails and break free.

Time I don't have.

The timer clicks as the red numbers staring back at me roll over to eight minutes. The sound of rushed feet and a slammed door is my cue.

Click...

Eight minutes...

"I don't have a lot of time." My voice is laced with tension. I'm literally up against a ticking clock, there's no time for fake pleasantries and bullshit conversation. I'm not a man of many words anyway. "I found the guy we've been tracking, but he caught me. The room I'm in is rigged with a bomb, and it's unlike anything I've ever seen before."

"Alright, Backdraft, tell us everything you see," Hashtag says, picking up on the severity of what I'm telling them.

"The bomb's in a metal box, surrounded by wires and some kind of electronic panel. There's a digital timer counting down on the top." I speak as clearly as I can, given the fact that my heart is thudding in my throat. For a man who thrives on chaos and chasing the adrenaline high, I'm riding an all-time low right now as the timer clicks yet again with its warning I'm running out of time.

Click…

Seven…

"What color are the wires? Can you see any markings?"

"It's a jumble of red, black, and yellow wires. No markings or labels, and there's a mix of thin and thick wires."

Click…

Six minutes…

I can hear Hashtag furiously pounding at the keys on his laptop.

Click…

Five minutes…

"Okay, listen carefully. We need to find the main power source and disable it. Look for a thick, black wire. It should be connected to a battery or power supply."

Click…

Four minutes…

I'm all thumbs and fat fingers as I walk them down and around the wires, tracing each one until I locate the one matching his description. "Got it. I see the thick black wire connected to a battery pack."

"That's the one," Hashtag confirms. "Now, we need to trace the path of the other wires to see which one is connected to the detonator. Can you see a yellow wire leading away from the timer?"

Click…

Three minutes…

"Yes, there's a yellow wire going from the timer to a small metal box."

"That's the detonator," Hashtag declares. "We need to cut that wire without triggering the bomb. Take a deep breath, Backdraft. You've got this."

Click…

Two minutes…

I wipe the sweat from my forehead and inhale a deep breath. This is the life or death high I've spent most of my life chasing but if I'm honest with myself, I prefer not death. "Alright, I'm ready."

Flicking my blade open, I grip the wire between my thumb and forefinger with my left hand and press the sharp steel to the plastic casing with my right. One last deep breath and I slice through the wire just as the digital display rolls over again.

Click…

One minute…

"Talk to us, Backdraft." Aero barks through the crackling interference on the line.

"I got it." A heavy rush of breath rolls over the blood on my lips when the timer freezes. If it weren't for my Club, my brothers, my family, I'd be a dead man right now.

As foreign as those words taste on my tongue, I've never meant anything more. Until the call from Jameson that a new chapter was forming in Atlantic City and he wanted me to meet with Aero for the position of Enforcer, I thought I was destined to roam the open roads alone. A man with scars as deep as mine is made to walk with the shadows. A face like this can kill.

Now that I've bought myself another day, that's exactly what I'll do. Locate my target and take every one of these punk-ass motherfuckers to the ground.

Chapter 2
Zoey

The heat of the sun beats down on my skin as I stretch my feet out on the lush green grass at the edge of the blanket. Setting my book aside, I turn my face upward to the sky, basking in its rays and inhaling the fragrant flowers that dot the open field for as far as my eyes can see. A gentle breeze brushes against my skin, offering a brief reprieve from the heat, but it also carries the uneasy feeling of eyes on me. Eyes that are always watching me. There's no escape from the darkness that lurks behind his black eyes, constantly boring into my flesh. Even out here, yards away from his watchful stare.

"You shouldn't be out here." I freeze as Justin moves in behind me interrupting my solitude. His shadow looms over me, casting a dark blanket over the sunshine. His voice sends chills down my arms, despite the heat of the sultry summer day beating down on me.

"I'm just enjoying the sunshine." I contest his argument and move into a less vulnerable position. Fear floods through my veins being caught off guard and alone with him. "It's a beautiful day and I'm tired of being cooped up in the house."

Justin kneels in front of me, the stale beer on his breath fans over my face, overpowering the sweet scent of summer flowers and freshly cut grass. His hair is cropped short and his face is hard with a constant scowl etched onto his features. "The view is spectacular," he eyes me up and down, "but your father will have my ass if he catches you disobeying his orders again."

A sneer tugs at his lips, twisting them up into an unsettling grin. I walked right into that.

Justin has been a constant presence in my life for as long as I can remember, serving as my father's right-hand man. His loyalty to my father is unquestionable, evident by his missing right hand, but his watchful eyes and controlling ways have always made me uneasy. He is dedicated to keeping this place running smoothly, but he also takes it upon himself to track my every move. I have no interest in a relationship with him or any man here, but that only adds to the loneliness. My father's group is tight knit. He doesn't take too well to company and I can't remember ever seeing a woman other than me around. I've learned to keep my thoughts and emotions guarded, knowing the inevitable heartache that comes with being a part of this solitary life.

Justin's warning confuses me. I'm normally free to move about unchaperoned as long as I stay within the set perimeter that my father has established for me. This stretch of open field is pushing those boundaries but it's quiet out here. Peaceful even. A welcome change from the metallic smells of the lab and bunkhouses.

Acres of green grass stretch out for miles covered with patches of wildflowers, the bright colors a stark contrast to the realities of this place. Further away, the trees sway gently in the breeze, providing a peaceful backdrop. Behind that, a steep rocky cliff keeps me in and the outside world out. The scenery is broken up only by the scattered scraps of rusted metal and abandoned vehicles surrounding an old storage unit looming in the distance.

This spot has become a refuge from the harsh reality I live in. A place I can lose myself in my daydreams. In my mind, I'm rescued by a mysterious stranger and whisked away to freedom and whatever lies beyond this place. Here, within these walls, no man can break through the impenetrable barrier of my father's control. If my father has his way, I'll spend the rest of my existence trapped in this compound until I either break or the world collapses into chaos at his hands.

I swallow back the bitterness and unease in my mouth as I try to stay composed in front of Justin. It's a flavor I've become all too familiar with in his presence. "Why? Is there something happening?"

Justin's toothy grin snaps into a tight scowl and his hand closes around my wrist in a vice grip that's so tight it will leave a bruise. "When is that ever your business?"

"It's… It's not." My voice cracks in response. I know better than to ask questions but there's an uneasiness in the air today. The activity around the compound is unusually active.

It's been seven years since my father brought me here and built this place from the ground up. But even now, weeks shy of my twenty-first birthday, my father still sees me as naive and unaware of what goes on around here. On the surface, it's a pretty mask disguising the true nature of my father's sadistic ways. Growing up within these walls, off the grid and hidden from prying eyes, I've become all too familiar with the harsh realities of this world. The sound of explosions and the sight of men missing fingers or limbs, like Justin, are all too common occurrences. Although my father tries to shelter me from that part of his world, it's always in the forefront. It's a constant reminder of the violence that lurks behind the beauty of this place.

"Take yourself home now," Justin orders me. "I'll be up later to check on you."

"Fine. I'm going." I huff and roll my eyes. When he breaks his hold on my wrist, my spine stiffens, "But don't bother. I don't want to see you."

My movements are slow as I gather up the blanket and the book I was reading into my arms. A storm rages behind his dark eyes. I've pissed him off good this time. His lips part but before he can respond, a voice comes through the walkie on his hip biding me a reprieve.

His eyes narrow on me as he draws the walkie to his mouth, "All clear on the East."

I turn away from him, leaving him to his rounds. When I no longer feel his eyes watching me, I toss a glance over my shoulder as he slips into the tree line running the length of the property.

My normal obedient temperament shatters like glass in his wake. I don't appreciate his tone or being told what to do by a man that makes my skin crawl. In my insolence, my gaze strays to the storage unit, and while every instinct in my body tells me to stay clear of whatever is going on, there's a rebel voice within dying to burst free that overpowers them all. I let my inner rebel loose for the first time in my life, hauling myself away from the path back to the main house and toward the rickety old shed that Justin seemed to have his focus on when it wasn't glued to me. I don't have a plan, supplies, or an inkling of how to pull this off but that will not stop me this time. To hell with them all. I hate this life and I refuse to let it break me. There's more to this life than what's in store for me here. There must be a way out and I will find it.

The sound of rumbling thunder heading down the gravel road takes me by surprise. In a panic, I duck down into knee-high weeds to hide behind a rusty old truck propped up with cinder blocks. Sweat from the afternoon sun beads at the back of my neck while I'm crouched low against the heap of hot, crumpled metal hiding me from view. Burrs jab into my ankles making me wish I was wearing something to protect my feet and legs other than the long white sundress I chose this morning when I thought I'd be alone with my thoughts and a good book instead of making a break for it. The sound grows louder as a convoy of trucks pass by, the weight of their cargo crunching their tires along the gravel road. Inhaling a sharp breath, I wait them out. With nothing to do but let my mind wander, a new fear fills me. I don't know who these people are, but I know nothing good can come with the amount of explosives they're moving off the compound.

After several minutes, the convoy clears out and the air around me grows silent, all but the thudding of my heart. I let go of the breath I'm holding, only to realize the dull pounding isn't coming from my chest. Following the sound, I move closer to the storage unit, careful to stay out of view if Justin or anyone else wanders by. In a few short strides, I'm close enough to lean in and press my ear to the wood. The distinct sound of pounding and shuffling feet coming from the other side of the wall is clear. There's someone inside.

If I had any sense of self-preservation, I'd turn away and hurry back to the main house where I belong. Instead, I cling to the remnants of curiosity that's gotten me this far, despite the fear growing in my gut. I barely make out the muffled voice on the other side because I'm already standing at the door with my fingers wrapped around a rusted metal rod found among the scraps.

With trembling hands, I wedge the rod into the gap between the door and the jamb. Its sharp and jagged edges bite into my palms as I pry the door open with all my strength. The wood groans in protest, splinters flying as the door gives way and his gruff voice hits my ears and steals my breath.

"Don't move."

Chapter 3
Backdraft

Inspecting the door frame, I search along the old, worn boards for weak spots. My hands scour over the rough edges, lodging sharp splinters into the tips of my fingers. Kicking at the boards, dirt flies into the air but gives way to a hole just big enough for my hand. Reaching inside, I pry the boards apart. Working them back and forth until the rusty nails start to pop. The rotting wood snaps in my hands and slivers of wood break away opening the hole wider.

Through the newly formed gap, a pair of white flip-flops catch my attention. At first, I think my eyes are playing tricks on me from the intense heat. But then, I see them again. A pair of white flip-flops, delicate soft feet with pink polish on the toes are standing on the other side of the wall, a mere inch from my fingertips. I blink rapidly, trying to determine if it's a real person or a hallucination when something hard wedges between the door and the frame, knocking me off balance. I stumble back on my heels and that's when I notice a thin wire, almost invisible to the naked eye glinting in the light and sneaking in through the newly made crevices. The wire is cleverly twisted around the door hinges and runs along the floorboard, blending in with the dark wood. I carefully grasp the wire in my hand following its trail back to the bomb. My heart is racing in my chest when the wire draws taunt in my hand. The pestilent click of the timer echoes through the space, reverberating off the walls in rapid-fire tics. The sound, a warning of impending danger, sends a shiver down my spine. The moment the door flies open, my instincts roar to life and my body reacts before I have time to think about it.

"Don't move," I shout, propelling myself through the door, hoisting the woman over my shoulders as I bolt into a clearing just as the bomb detonates.

A deafening explosion reverberates through the air, shaking the ground beneath my feet. A wave of searing heat and flames erupt, launching me forward with a violent force. The ringing in my ears is disorienting and I stumble over my big feet landing us both on the ground with a hard smack. Covering her with my body, I shield her from the shards of wood and debris raining down around us. The heat from the blast warms my skin in a familiar way. For a split second,

I am blinded by the bright orange light that engulfs everything. I blink my eyes and clear my focus.

The moment I open my eyes, she appears below me like a mirage. Soot smears across the delicate fabric of her long white sundress, creating a stark contrast against her pale features. Her eyes, a mesmerizing gold that reflects the dancing yellow and orange flames around us, hold a haunting beauty. Ashes drift down from above, cascading around her like snowflakes caressing the skin of a porcelain angel and darkening the loose golden strands of her hair. The thick smoke has me in a choke hold as I take in the surreal sight before me. Her full lips are slightly parted and her eyes wide with shock as we stand up and take it all in. Instead of looking at me, her eyes ping-pong at the destruction around us. She's taking in the chaos and I can't tell if she's fearful or in awe of the beauty in the destruction. Most people compartmentalize the world into the good, the bad, and the ugly. Choosing to live only in the good space where they can hide their eyes and pretend the rest doesn't exist. That's where they feel safe, maybe even bored, but the same people cram their necks to watch as tragedy unfolds. Then they quickly file it away, hidden under prayers and well wishes. They fail to see that even destruction holds beauty. Chaos is a high, one that once you get a taste of it, it's hard to ignore.

I watch her take it all in and wonder what it is she sees. For a minute there's a flash in her eyes that makes me wonder if she sees it like I do. When her eyes finally draw to mine, she swallows hard. I watch as the lump slowly works its way down her throat and my mind wanders to a place it has no business going.

"Who are you?" she asks, her voice as hypnotic as the rest of her features.

The way the sound filters through my ears sends a shooting sensation straight to my dick. I store it in my memory for later. Now is not the time to see how far into my world I can drag this angel before it burns her alive. I have a job to do.

Sometimes, tracking a target takes skill honed over years. Other times, like this one, fate intercedes. I don't know how or why she ended up in the path of the blast meant to kill me, but she's within reach and now I have to get her out of here.

"I'll explain later, Zoey. We have to go now." As soon as her name pours out of my mouth, she stumbles backward. Confusion draws her sweet face tight. There's no time to tell her what I know or why I'm here. We're about to have company.

I look out over her shoulder and see several figures moving closer. It's only a matter of time until they realize I cleared the blast and it won't take them much longer to figure out I have her.

She opens her mouth and a scream rips from her throat when a bullet zips past us. I tug her down as another shot rips over our heads.

Her hands, so soft and small, smack against my chest. "Get away from me."

Her voice rises as she continues to scream, drawing even more unwanted attention our way. I press my hand over her mouth, muffling her scream, "Shh. I'm trying to help you."

Zoey struggles under my hold, sinking her teeth into my skin. I jerk my hand away from her mouth and she screams again. "Help me? I've been near you for less than five minutes and I've already been blown up and now I'm being shot at by my own family. I don't need help this bad."

I can't stop the smirk from spreading across my face, which only seems to make her angrier. She may seem docile at first glance, but given the right circumstances she could be dangerous, and that has my blood pumping.

My nonchalant demeanor is quickly replaced with a hard stare, "I don't recall offering you a choice."

Rising voices, rushed movements, and more gunfire aimed in our direction drown out any response she might have. I scan our surroundings and assess what's left in the debris. There's not much to work with. The blast took out anything that would provide cover nearby. That's when I remember my ace in the hole, assuming it's still within range. Retrieving my phone from my pocket, I grimace at the damage. Cracks spider web across the screen from landing on it in the wake of the explosion. I unlock the screen and locate the programmed number that will trigger the remote charge in the cap bomb. The screen flickers intermittently, displaying fractured lines of text but despite the damage it connects. Seconds later, ripple detonations erupt from somewhere off in the distance. Followed by an unexpectedly larger blast with a visceral force that shakes the tops of the trees in the distance. The impromptu distraction divides the men heading in our direction, giving me a fighting chance.

Chapter 4
Zoey

The deafening sounds of bullets whipping past my head fill the air. Their sharp cracks ring out and bounce off the remnants of the debris surrounding me. Each shot is like a burst of thunder, sending shockwaves through my body as I duck for cover. But it's not the danger and confusion that has my heart pounding. It's the imposing figure of the man standing over me. His intense gaze and steady stance exudes power and control, sending a chill down my spine, and making my blood run cold despite the heat of the flames still burning around us.

Sweat beads on my temples as I struggle to catch my breath. The acrid smell of burning wood and fear hangs heavy in the air as I try to make sense of the situation, unsure if this man is a savior or a threat. Everything about him is shrouded in darkness, from his jet-black hair to his vacant slate-gray eyes that seem to pierce through me. His heavy goatee and bronze skin only add to the intensity surrounding me. Even his voice rumbles like thunder, exuding a sense of danger that should frighten me. His long legs are encased in tight black jeans, leading to a broad chest that strains against the shirt and leather vest he's wearing.

As our eyes meet, his dark gaze bores into mine with an unspoken challenge. I can feel his heated gaze reddening my cheeks and making me squirm in my skin. I should turn and run away from him, back to the enemy I know, but instead I find myself drawn to him for reasons I can't put my finger on. My eyes graze over the leather vest he's wearing, adorned with patches. I'm transfixed on the intricate black and white design of a menacing skull with a long beard flowing down from its chin and wearing a crown. On either side of the skull are motorcycles emblazoned with wings. I speak the words silently in my head as I read the words embedded above it: Royal Bastards MC, and below it, Atlantic City NJ. The gritty, distressed look gives it a rebellious and rugged vibe that suits the man standing before me. My eyes continue to move over him until they land on another patch that reads Backdraft.

"Backdraft?" I speak out loud without even realizing it. "Is that your name?"

"Yes," is all he says before another round of gunfire flies past us and ricochets off the remnants of the shed now strewn around us in pieces.

Backdraft grabs my arm, forcing me to move with him again. I grit out my discontent but there's no real force behind it. There's no way my father and his men haven't noticed me clutching onto this man for my life and yet they continue to move in on us, not caring that I'm trapped in the crossfire.

I hate being Dominic Cassedy's daughter. I hate the confines he puts on me and I hate being hidden away in this fucking place, but my father is supposed to protect me. Justin, though unwanted, has always done the same. So why am I suddenly at the wrong end of their wrath? Nothing about this day or what I've seen makes any sense.

"We have to move. Are you with me or not?" Backdraft snaps his fingers in my face, breaking me from the thoughts scattering around in my head.

I have a choice to make but only one gets me my freedom. I will never find that here, not while my father and Justin run things. I accepted that fact a long time ago. While this may have started as a temper tantrum, it's now the only way I see to get out of here. Unless it gets me killed first. My argument dies on my tongue and I reach out in surrender. Backdraft takes me by the hand, his grip firm and comforting.

I peek over his shoulder, my heart racing at the distinct rumble of a dirt bike. The engine roars like an angry animal, tearing through the chaos as it approaches. Backdraft turns his head following my gaze at the same time I do.

A thick trail of dust and debris explodes into the air, leaving a hazy wake in its path. The smell of gasoline and burnt rubber mix with the pungent smell in the air as it hurtles past us. In a split second, the rider is on top of us. His outstretched arm snatches mine as he passes by. He forcefully jerks me backward towards him. The pain in my arm shoots through my body like electricity, radiating through my shoulder and lodging into my neck before the bike skids out from underneath him. I struggle to catch my breath as he grips onto me tightly as if I'm the threat. At the same time, he pulls a gun from his pocket and aims at Backdraft.

Tension coils in Backdraft's body as he grips the gun in his hand. With his finger poised on the trigger with deadly precision, he aims. Backdraft's jaw sets in a determined line and his eyes burn with a fierce intensity as the two men lock in a standoff with me in between.

"Back off," he growls. "She's ours."

I have never felt more like a piece of property than I do at this moment. I'd like to say the years that I have been here have been filled with love and kindness from my father and his crew, but I'd be lying to myself. None of them have ever harmed me physically, but I've always been in the way more than anything else. The only declaration of love shown to me is from Justin and that's more possession than love. The thought saddens me and stirs emotions I've locked away for years. There's more tenderness in the darkness glowering in Backdraft's eyes than I've ever seen from them.

Backdraft's eyes narrow as he glares at the man whose death grip is bruising my arm.

"Over my dead body," Backdraft snaps. "She's coming with me."

Backdraft's declaration snaps something inside of me. I turn, swinging my arm until my fist slams into the side of his face. His grip breaks and I fly toward Backdraft before he can get his hands on me again. At the same time, Backdraft's finger curls around the trigger.

There's no real sound as the gun recoils. Yet my head feels like a thousand bells are clanging at once in my ear, reverberating through my entire body. I struggle to keep my footing. I reach out and grab onto Backdraft. His large arms wind around me, holding me upright. With a snarl curling his lips, his deep voice rumbles through his chest and slams into my own. "Do what I say, when I say it, or neither of us is getting out of here."

All I can do is nod. As soon as his arms let me go, all I want to do is crawl back into them.

"Get behind me," Backdraft demands, pulling me around his side until his back is shielding me. Releasing the empty magazine from the clip, he shoves a new one in and slams the base into his palm to lock it in place.

When he starts firing again, it's as if something snaps inside of him. There's no dodging for cover, no hesitation. He unleashes a round of bullets, coating the crisp green field red. The roars ripping out of his chest rumble deep into my bones as he fires. I can't stop the tears from leaking out of the corners of my eyes as one by one they all drop. My insides twist into knots. I want to be free, and I can't deny the lust coiling my system for the beast shielding me, but I wasn't prepared for the emotions that overtake me as I watch the men I have spent most of my life with pay for my unhappiness with their lives.

When the only ones left standing are the two of us, Backdraft tucks his gun at his side and turns around. I've never seen eyes so cold as his glare meets mine. I'm not even sure he can see me through the cloud he's under but his stare burns into me.

With a sharp flick of his wrist, he snaps a knife out from under his vest. The bright sunlight glints off the metal blade, flashing in my eyes and temporarily skewing my line of sight. When my eyes clear, his cold gaze is locked onto mine. My heart is racing under the trail of the blade as he drags the tip of the knife down my chest. I can't pull my eyes from the gleaming blade as he draws it lower along my stomach and then my thighs. Goosebumps shoot across my body as I watch, both terrified and turned on at the same time.

Something dark and primal flashes in his eyes and my breath catches in my throat. With a sly grin, he slices the blade through the fabric of my dress just above my knees. With his other hand, he rips the material with such force the shredded material of my dress flutters to the ground at my feet. His rough hands brush against my bare skin and waves of heat pulse throughout my body.

"Spread your legs, Little Lamb," he commands with a deep rumble in his voice, "and get on the bike."

He climbs on first, holding it upright between his powerful thighs, and reaches out his arm. With shaky legs, I swing one over and settle onto the seat behind him. He turns the gas and forcefully kickstarts the engine. The dirt bike revs to life with a deep growl vibrating the seat underneath me. Standing upright, he leans forward gripping the handlebars.

"Hold on tight, Little Lamb. It's gonna be a bumpy ride."

Shifting closer, I press my body against his back, wrapping my arms tightly around him. He calls me Little Lamb. Why does that make me feel like I'm being led to the slaughter?

Chapter 5
Backdraft

Adrenaline rushes through my system as I kick the piece of shit dirt bike to life. I've taken out everyone in our way and the only thing I can think about at this moment is getting Zoey out of this Godforsaken place. The girl has no idea who she is or why she was brought here. I'm just grateful there's fire in her eyes and she seems to know there's more for her than the life she's living here. That makes my job easier. These bastards haven't broken her spirit yet, but I can't be sure that the Bastard she's holding onto won't.

Her slender arms grip my waist in a death grip. Sweat beads along my body and drips down my back but she doesn't seem to care. She's trusting me with her life and I won't let her down.

I curse under my breath, my hold on the handlebars tightening. My thighs burn from riding standing up, but I race down the rough terrain. The wind whips past us as I push the throttle as far as it will go. I watch as the plume overhead gets closer and hear the loud voices up ahead. It's then I realize what I've done when I spot the burning truck and a body face down in the dirt on the side of the road. The destruction my cap bomb caused is more than I could have bargained for, which makes me wonder what was in those trucks and hits me this fight has just gotten a whole lot dirtier. I'm now up against two enemies. I commit what I can see of the Asphalt Gods MC patch to memory and make a hard right. The dirt bike tears through the grass to carve a new path. The groans of dirt bikes and all-terrain vehicles grow louder behind us. They're in hot pursuit, firing wildly into the air.

With the wind pushing against us, I lean into the bike pushing it to its limits. Zoey's arms tighten around my waist as the adrenaline surges through me. Glancing over my shoulder, I see them gaining on us, their engines grinding trying to keep up the pace. Without my motorcycle, we can't outrun them forever. This dirt bike can't perform with the power and speed I'm used to. I'm a skilled rider but we can't keep this up much longer.

Taking a risk, I steer us off the worn path and into a stretch of woods, crashing through the underbrush. We race through the trees, dodging branches and obstacles in our path. The sound of their engines die out and I breathe a small sigh of relief, although I know this is far from over. Zoey is not safe yet. As we race through the woods, I can feel Zoey's heartbeat racing against my back. The adrenaline coursing through my veins dulls the pain in my shoulder from where I had been shot earlier. But now is not the time to think about that. I focus on navigating through the thick trees and shrubs, trying to find a way out of this maze. I push the bike faster, my heart pounding in my chest as I try to anticipate which direction will lead us to safety.

An unexpected bump sends us flying. Zoey and I roll to the ground, our bodies skidding down the side of a steep hill. Branches tug at my clothing. Sharp rocks rip into my flesh. I dig my legs into the dirt trying to slow my speed so my ass doesn't go over the embankment. Stretching my arms out, I catch Zoey as she skids down the rough terrain, her small body flopping around like a rag doll. When she crashes into me, I wrap my arms around her pulling her out of the path of the dirt bike skidding down behind us. The bike shoots by us and soars over the edge. We finally skid to a stop, slamming into a large tree. I pull her closer, leaning against the rough bark. Her small frame is trembling against me and I can feel her heart racing. I tighten my grip on her, trying to provide some comfort and stability. My breathing is hard and fast, my heart slamming against my chest. I inhale slowly, urging Zoey to do the same.

"Breathe with me, Little Lamb. I've got you."

She's hyperventilating and I have to get her under control before we can move. My hands are dirty and calloused, but I'm gentle when gripping Zoey's hand and guiding it to my chest so she can feel the slow, steady breaths I take.

"That's it. In and out."

Zoey's breathing gradually slows down as she mimics my controlled inhales and exhales. After a few minutes, Zoey calms down enough for us to move. I grunt as we slowly get up, my body aching from the fall. Looking her over, she's covered in dirt and scratches. I brush the leaves from the remnants of her sundress, thankful she didn't fall off the edge. Sweeping my hands over her torn flesh, she winces as I brush a gash on her arm.

"You're okay," I reassure her while I continue to search for injuries. I'm not a gentle man and it takes all the strength I have to be tender with my touch.

She's visibly shaken from the fall, but I'm confident she didn't endure any serious injuries by the time I reach her feet. When I spot the soft pink hue on her toes, anger with myself roars inside my chest but I keep it locked inside.

How could I forget she wasn't wearing proper shoes?

I help her sit back down and kneel to untie my leather boots. The worn laces slide easily through my fingers as I unstrap them. I slip them off and carefully ease them onto her bare feet.

"I can't take your boots." She argues with me but quickly gives up when I don't acknowledge her protest.

Letting her take another moment to collect herself, I glance around trying to figure out which direction to go. To the right, I spot a worn path through the trees. It's overgrown with weeds, but it's made to lead somewhere. I contemplate taking it. It would be the easiest route for Zoey and possibly lead us to somewhere safe to rest while I figure out our next move, but I can't shake the feeling in my gut that the easy choice is the wrong choice.

Scanning our surroundings, I spot one of her flip-flops half-buried in the loose dirt a short distance away. Zoey's gaze is fixed on my every move as I stalk over and pick it up. I walk toward the edge and toss the sandal over, watching as it tumbles down the jagged rocks before landing on a ledge jetting out below. Reaching into the pocket of my vest, my fingers close around my supplies. I assemble another cap bomb but this time I spare the detonator. Instead, I ignite it. My fingers work quickly as I strike the match and nestle it between the clay pieces before launching it into the air. The explosion that echoes through the air will get their attention, but it should also draw them away from the path we'll make.

"We need to keep moving," I help Zoey up. "Be careful, the ground is uneven."

Taking Zoey's small hand in mine and a broken tree branch in the other, we veer off in the opposite direction away from the beaten trail. Trailing the jagged tree branch across the ground behind us, I brush away our footprints until we're safely out of sight.

Surrounded by the dense woods, I release the branch, letting it fall to the ground. Guided by instinct, I lead Zoey through the underbrush, deliberately moving in the opposite direction from where I've led them to search. The thick canopy above casts patchy shadows around us as we tread carefully through the trees, every step taking us deeper.

Chapter 6
Zoey

As we push through the thick underbrush and dense trees, our progress is slow. The jagged terrain is an obstacle course of roots and fallen branches. My hand trembles in his, his grip tightening with each uneven step. I'm scared, but I'm doing my best to keep up with his long strides without tripping over my feet in his too-large boots.

I steal a glance at our intertwined hands, comforted by how his larger fingers envelop mine. His worn socks are covered in dirt and dried leaves. A sigh breaks loose, thinking about the gesture. No one has ever done anything as selfless for me before.

"Are you okay?" Backdraft asks, breaking the silence between us. He glances back at me briefly with a hint of concern in his eyes.

"Yes," I answer, trying to sound more confident than I feel.

We walk for miles until we finally emerge into a small clearing. The sun is setting, casting an orange glow over an old, weathered structure standing alone on a hill in the distance. It looks like it hasn't been inhabited in a while, with peeling white paint clinging stubbornly to the wooden boards. The patchwork of darker timber and mismatched shingles shows its history of hasty repairs. The grass surrounding it is overgrown and shadowed by tall trees stretching their limbs out overhead adding to the eerie feeling. Backdraft's steps falter when he sees it too, uncertainty flickering across his face.

"Is it safe?" I ask, my voice barely above a whisper.

"I don't know," he replies, his brow furrowed. "But it's getting dark and we need shelter."

He leads us cautiously towards the cabin, our footsteps crunching on dried leaves and twigs. We pass a rusty, green pickup truck and a neatly stacked pile of firewood before we ascend the creaky wooden stairs to the front porch. Windows dot the small hunting cabin, some crooked and unevenly placed and others boarded up. They're mostly dark and obscured by dirt and cobwebs, but through the dull glass by the door, I can make out the thin line of curtains draped inside. The small detail brings me some comfort, knowing someone lives here or at least uses it as an escape from time to time. Luckily for us, it looks like no one is here now. Curling his hand around the doorknob, Backdraft jiggles the handle only to find it locked. Pulling something plastic from under his vest, he wedges it between the door and the frame, sliding it up and down until the lock pops open.

"Stay close to me," he orders in a deep low tone that sends shivers down my spine.

"I will," I reply, my voice barely above a whisper.

Retrieving his gun, he slowly pushes on the rickety door. It creaks in protest. Backdraft takes one step inside, sweeping the room from left to right, and then takes another. I follow his lead, staying close behind him.

Our footsteps echo through the space. The air inside is damp and musty, making me crinkle my nose in disgust. I push through it, taking in my surroundings. The only light is what's left of the sun streaming through the open door and the dirty windows, casting an eerie glow along the floorboards. The structure is weakened from age and lack of upkeep, but it has the basic necessities from what I can tell. The main room is cluttered with old furniture and various items strewn about. There's a worn-out couch against one wall, a dusty table with chairs next to it, a wood-burning stove, and a kitchenette area with a sink and stove on the other side.

Backdraft turns his eyes searching mine for any signs of discomfort or fear. I give him a small nod, letting him know that I'm okay. After everything he's done for me already, I'd follow him anywhere.

He hands me his cell phone, "Take this."

The weak beam of light from the flashlight app casts long shadows on the worn wooden floor as we cautiously make our way through the cabin. I cling to his shirt as he leads us further into the cabin. Pausing at a door, he slowly opens it revealing a small bedroom. A single twin bed sits against one wall, surrounded by a chair and a small nightstand. To the side is a closet, its door slightly ajar revealing a few items still inside. Next to that door is another. Backdraft opens it into a tiny bathroom with peeling wallpaper and a cracked mirror.

When he's confident the place is empty, he returns his gun to his side and turns. "We'll stay here for the night."

Exhaustion starts to catch up with me, the adrenaline draining from my body and leaving me feeling tired and sore. I sink onto the edge of the bed, running my hand over my bare legs. Backdraft rummages through the room and comes to stand in front of me, powering on a battery-powered lantern and setting it on the floor at my feet. The soft glow illuminates the cuts and bruises on my skin.

"Let me see," Backdraft says, kneeling in front of me.

I nod, too exhausted to protest. He works quickly unlacing the strings of the boots. With a gentle tug, he slips them off my feet and places them at the foot of the bed. His fingers trace over every wound from my toes up my legs, sending shivers down my spine. Goosebumps erupt on my flesh from the heat of his touch. I flinch when his hand grazes over a large bruise blooming on my inner thigh.

He gazes at me, his eyes smoldering with a dark hunger. His hand roams freely over my exposed skin, setting every nerve ablaze with a raw need for him to explore deeper. The electric current that jolts through my entire being ignites a fire within me that I can't control.

Backdraft's hand pauses, dangerously close to my soaking-wet panties. I'm practically squirming with anticipation. My heart races as he stops just as his fingers skim the edge. Stealing a glance at him, I see he's covered in cuts and bruises of his own. Old burns and scars mark his tanned skin, but they don't scare me.

"You're hurt." I reach for him, returning the same gentleness he's shown me.

A look flashes in his eyes, telling me that's not the response he expected. There's more to him than what's on the surface. I can see it in his eyes. The danger, the secrets hidden behind them. He's been through some heavy-hitting stuff, but when it comes to me, he's been a gentle giant.

"It's just part of the job," he brushes off my concern, abruptly pulling away.

I swallow hard, trying to ignore the fluttering in my stomach. As he moves around the room, I'm aware of every small detail. The subtle creaking of the floorboards beneath his weight, the warmth radiating from his body, and the faint sound of our breathing.

"What are you looking for?"

"A change of clothes."

I glance down at what's left of the sundress I'm wearing, realizing that it's dirty, bloodstained, and torn to shreds. Backdraft rummages through the dresser drawers and then the closet, finally finding what he's looking for.

"This is all I can find, but it's clean." He places the clothes on the bed next to me.

"Thank you." I place my hand on the pile, grazing his as he pulls it away.

"I need to secure the perimeter before it gets too dark." The resounding thud of the door shutting behind him jolts me out of the hypnotic state I'd fallen under and frustration crawls across my skin.

Chapter 7
Backdraft

I make a quick exit from the bedroom with my cock rock-hard against the zipper of my jeans. Given the circumstances, touching her is off limits but I couldn't help myself. It started as a way to access her injuries, but as my fingers grazed over her skin, something came over me. I was possessed by her intoxicating scent and the pure sweetness radiating off her. Everything about her from her long blonde hair, those rich amber eyes, all the way down to those damn pink toenails has me tied in knots.

When my hand grazed the hem of her panties, I could feel her arousal. She was wet and aching for my touch. It took all the self-restraint I could muster to stop myself from exploring further. When she touched me back, reminding me of the burns and scars covering my body, darkness clouded my judgment. I expected her to withdraw like women usually do but that wasn't fear I saw in her eyes. It was something else. Lust, need, hunger... Sure, club whores will drop to their knees in front of me and even fuck me. That's what they do, though. Doesn't mean I don't see the way they look at me, like I'm damaged. And they're right. I am. Inside and out. I have the mental and physical scars to prove it. A body like this is hard to love. Hell, I was hard to love before the burns. They serve as a reminder of how fucked up I am. I'm no good for her, even if she couldn't see it at that moment.

The look on her face when I pushed her away was like a knife to the heart, but it had to be done. It doesn't matter how bad I want her. My job was to locate her and return her to the people who hired us, not fuck her along the way. Damn, I need to get my head on straight. She needs my protection, not my corruption.

With heavy steps, I stalk out of the front door of the cabin and make my way towards the woodpile by the stairs. I can't help but think about the way her thighs clutched around my hips while we were on the stolen dirt bike. Which leads to picturing her riding bitch on my motorcycle, her tits pressed against my back and her arms wrapped tightly around my waist. My cock is hard again and I give it a tug in my pants to reposition myself. Damn, this woman is already getting to me. Being stuck here and keeping my wits about me is going to be rough.

Shaking off my thoughts, I gather logs into my arms, the dry rough bark digging into my skin and bringing me clarity as to what I am supposed to be doing. The sun has set by the time I step back inside and my discomfort is nowhere near eased. I toss the bundle into the wood-burning stove and rip scraps of magazine pages from the nearby table, arranging them beneath the logs. Flicking my lighter, I watch as the blue melds into orange. My fingertips slice through the flame and it dances on my skin until the heat singes my fingers. Then I lower it to the kindling. It doesn't take long for the flame to catch, rising and taking shape before my eyes.

The crackling of the flames and the popping of burning wood echo in my ears, drowning out everything else. I focus on the steady rhythm of my breath. The sound of air filling my lungs and leaving my body does nothing to ease the ache inside me. The sound of water running drags my focus away. Before I know what I'm doing, I'm pushing through the bedroom door. The small room is suffocating as I stare at her through the partially opened bathroom door. Her reflection in the mirror teases me, her naked body obscured by a dingy opaque shower curtain. I should look away, but I can't. I'm drawn to her like a flame. To the raw beauty of her body. My eyes trace down the curve of her spine, over the slope of her hips, and the swell of her ass. When she runs her hands through her wet hair and then across her breast trailing her fingers over her stomach and between her legs, I lose it.

Unable to stop myself, I pick her panties up from off the bed, bringing them to my nose and inhaling her scent. My eyes close as I lose control in the euphoria of her natural aroma. My pants tighten, my cock twitches. I unzip my jeans and free my aching cock, my hand grasping it tightly as I stroke. I imagine her body pressed against mine with each movement. I jerk and squeeze my cock as the heat builds inside me watching her getting herself off. My grip tightens as I pump relentlessly until I climax, releasing streams of cum into the delicate fabric twisting in my grip.

A low growl erupts from the depths of my throat. I stuff my cock back in my pants, storming from the room before she catches sight of the animal she's turning me into.

Chapter 8
Zoey

    With the lantern in my hand, I make my way into the other room. There's a chill from the evening mountain air creeping into the cabin but the warmth of the fire makes it tolerable. Unlike my mood. After Backdraft left me like he did, I had to take matters into my own hands. Literally, but even that did little to satisfy the throbbing between my legs caused by Backdraft's touch. The cold water didn't help matters either and now I'm going commando in a stranger's clothing because oddly enough I couldn't find my underwear. The t-shirt is so baggy that it hangs off my shoulders and the sweatpants are too wide, even with the drawstring pulled tight. At least the heavy socks are warm and comfortable.

    I stop in front of the wood-burning stove for a few minutes, letting the heat warm me and dry my hair. The bright orange flames flicker and dance, casting shadows across the dark cabin. Backdraft is nowhere to be found. I'm not sure if I'm relieved or disappointed. Maybe a mixture of both. I twist my hair up in a knot on top of my head and pad across the cold floor into the kitchenette area. Just as I expected, no Backdraft. Where the hell could he have gone? This place isn't big enough to hide. A chill runs over my bones but this time it's not from the air. The realization that he may have left me here alone after everything that has happened today is unsettling.

Anger surges through me, mixing with the hurt and betrayal already brewing inside of me. My hands shake as I reach for the refrigerator handle. I yank it open and confirm what I already suspected, no one has been here in months. The power is off, and the shelves are barren of food. The wretched smell hits my nostrils and I push the door closed. Reaching for a cupboard door I find a small ration of canned foods and a case of beer. Figuring I have nothing to lose, I twist the top and down a bottle in one gulp, trying to quell the panic rising in my chest. Its sharp, biting carbonation leaves a tingling sensation in its wake. I scrunch my face at the warm, bittersweet flavor that lingers on my tongue. Setting the empty bottle on the counter, I grab another. Pacing around the cabin, taking long swigs from the bottle every few minutes. My mind is racing with questions. Why did Backdraft leave me? Where did he go? Is he ever coming back? And most importantly, what am I going to do now?

Tears sting my eyes and I angrily swipe them away. Crying won't solve anything. At least not right now. I take another long drink from the bottle and my stomach drops when I see him through the window. The glow from his phone illuminates the worry on his face. He lifts it to his ear and then pulls it away, holds it out in front of him, and swipes it up in the air like he's trying to find a signal. Our eyes connect and it instantly pulls me back to him. His presence is so large and intrusive that it sucks the air from my lungs, suffocating me. I hate this feeling. I hate that I can't control the urges that rush through me when he's close to me and the crushing disappointment when he's not. He turns slightly, diverting his eyes from mine, and returns his focus to the phone in his hand.

"Good luck out here." I huff under my breath to myself. It's easy to live off the grid in the mountains for a reason. Cell phone reception is not reliable out here unless you're near a booster.

Taking another swig of beer, I flop down on the chair at the table, not wanting to admit the relief I feel that he's close by. Even if he might be trying to ignore me.

A cool whip of air fills the cabin when the door bursts open. The sudden impact makes me jump in my seat. I don't turn around or acknowledge him. He's the one who dragged me out here, teased me with his touch, and then bailed like I wasn't worth his time.

I feel him standing behind me, his scent filling my lungs and making me tense with the glare burning into my back. "Slow down, Little Lamb, I don't need you getting drunk on me."

My hand raises, bringing the glass to my lips and guzzling down what's left in the bottle. Backdraft takes a seat across from me, swiping the beer caps off the table and pocketing them into his vest. I glare at him, reaching for a third. I don't know why I'm acting this way. I'm accustomed to being told what to do but I'm sick and tired of it. I don't even know this man and he's been bossing me around from the start, like he owns me. Let's not forget that I saved his life. If it wasn't for me, he'd have blown up.

That realization makes my stomach churn. The bitter taste trails up the back of my throat. I can't stop the heave that rips out of my mouth and causes me to lunge forward in my chair. The overwhelming urge to vomit floods through me, threatening to spill out onto the floor. Backdraft's swift reflexes move a trash pail in front of me in time. The acrid smell of bile fills the air as I empty the contents of my stomach into the trash. My chest heaves with each retch, my entire body trembling.

"This is your fault." I huff out, slumping back into my seat, exhausted and embarrassed.

"Is that so? I forced you to pour warm beer down your throat?"

"No, but it's your fault those men are dead and I'm out here in the middle of nowhere instead of home in my own bed."

His head jerks up, darkness deepening the gray in his eyes. His teeth grind together, his nostrils flaring. "Let's get one thing straight here, Little Lamb. I didn't make you do shit. You chose to come with me, but I would have if you forced my hand."

I swallow hard, feeling the anger radiating off him, "And why is that? How is it you knew my name? What aren't you telling me?"

My breath hitches in my throat, when he shoves a glass of water in my face, "Drink."

I swing my arm out, pushing it away. "Stop telling me what to do and start telling me who you are and why I'm here."

"Drink the fucking water." He shoves the glass to my mouth with such force the water sloshes up the side and splashes over the edge onto my lips. Tipping my head back with his free hand, he pours the water down my throat. I gurgle and sputter as I struggle to swallow it. I cough and gasp for air as he pulls away, setting the empty glass on the table.

"Better?" he asks with a smirk, his hand still gripping my chin.

I nod, too afraid to speak. My mind is racing, trying to make sense of everything that's happened in this short amount of time. My heart is pounding in my chest, a mixture of fear and adrenaline coursing through me.

"Now," he releases me and sits back in his chair, crossing his arms over his chest, "what do you want to know?"

I take a deep breath, trying to steady myself before asking the questions again. "Who are you? How do you know who I am? And why am I here?"

He gives a low chuckle. "Well, Little Lamb, those are some loaded questions."

I glare at him. "I'm serious."

"So am I." He says with a serious expression on his face. "You know my name, it's Backdraft."

"That's not your real name," I retort.

He shrugs nonchalantly, "It's what everyone calls me."

I give up on that round of questioning and ask the more important one that's on my mind. "How do you know who I am?"

"I was hired to find you." His voice takes on an edge as he speaks.

"Hired by who?"

"That's not important right now."

"It's important to me!" I snap back.

He leans forward suddenly, his tone harsh, "Listen here, Little Lamb," he spits out with venom in his words. "You need to trust me."

My heart races as fear creeps into every fiber of my being. "You were hired to kidnap me and I'm supposed to trust you?"

"Retrieve you. Not kidnap you."

"Semantics." I push myself up from the chair and storm out of the room, realizing I'm not going to get anywhere with him.

He's behind me in a few long strides, closing in on me. With a force, his hands grip my shoulders. I whirl around to face him, furious tears threatening to spill over. My heart slams against my chest and my breathing kicks up a notch. This man is dangerous, but his touch does something to me. I have no idea what I've gotten myself into but I don't care. My hands dart up, gripping his huge biceps, that familiar need rushing through me again. His lips hover over mine, just a breath away. I lick my lips, my mouth suddenly dry. His eyes drop to my tongue and I swear a low growl rumbles his chest.

"What do we do now?"

Chapter 9
Backdraft

This isn't who I am. I don't make small talk or hash things out. Plans are for people with time to waste. I live by my own rules, fueled by adrenaline and instinct. But as I stare into her pleading eyes, I wish I could show her a different side of myself. One that's gentle and patient.

I drag my hand through my hair, ruffling the strands in frustration. I know I have to try for her or I'll regret it later. With a deep breath, I drag her down with me so we're sitting side by side on the worn-out couch. "We lay low for now and wait for backup."

"What if backup doesn't come?" Her voice is near a tremble.

"It will," I try to reassure her, even though I can't be sure of it without a signal. "As long as I have my phone, my club should be able to track me. In the meantime, I'll see if I can get that old truck out front started."

She gives a hesitant nod, but I can feel the tension in her body, every muscle tightly wound like a spring. Is she afraid they'll come after us and try to take her back? Or is she afraid of me?

"My name is Dax Shaw." I keep my voice low.

We sit in silence for a few minutes, lost in our thoughts. We watch the fire dance against the darkness, listening to it crackle and pop. As I steal a glance at her, I see the tension in her body slowly ease. She nestles closer to me, trusting and vulnerable. Without hesitation, I wrap my arm around her, pulling her even closer. The simple gesture is something I've never offered anyone before but somehow it feels right. When her head hits my shoulder, I don't move. I focus on her slow and steady breathing as she rests in my arms.

As I close my eyes, I can still see the bright orange flames of the fire dancing in my mind, a constant reminder of what I did. I see the smoke rising and the outlines of the trees and the house engulfed in the inferno.

I walk as one with the flames, moving towards them without fear or guilt. The flames stretch out like long fingers clawing and grabbing onto everything in its reach. The heat sears my skin, but I don't turn back. I can't. Not now. I need to see it. I need to see him.

With each step, my anger melds with the raging flames. I am consumed by the fierce embrace of the flames that lick at my skin, leaving trails of heat searing through me. The fire stretches out like a beast, its fiery fingers clawing at everything in its reach. It devours everything in its path with a hungry roar, but I do not fear it. Instead, I am drawn towards it, driven by a desperate need to see him. My determination is unyielding as I push forward, driven by an unexplainable force. And then I see him. Our eyes meet in a moment of understanding. That I am the cause. I am the reason fear drowns the usual rage that darkens his eyes and the flesh melts from his skin. His screams are silenced by the roaring inferno that crackles and roars around us. Its bright orange and red hues dance wildly. The air is thick with smoke and the sharp scent of burning wood. The corners of my lips draw upward as I stand amid the flames watching it consume him, reducing him to bone and ash.

My eyes snap open, my heart pounding with a ferocity that threatens to burst through my chest. The image of the man, the monster, sears into my mind as I gasp for air. My very being, twisted and corrupted by the touch of his memory, still bears the scars of his evil. And long after I've wiped away the sleep from my eyes, his final moments play on an endless loop in my mind. Even now, as I hold Zoey in my arms, I can still see the fear etched in his eyes, although it's been years since that moment. A moment that will always define who I am. A monster I have to constantly feed.

I steal a look at Zoey sleeping soundly in my arms, her innocence a light against the darkness within me. Having her body so close to mine awakens emotions I never knew existed, stirring a primal desire that both thrills and terrifies me. But I wonder how long it'll be until she realizes the truth about me and runs away in terror like all the others before her.

My muscles coil under my skin at the thought of losing her. Restlessness grasps hold of me like I need to keep moving or else I'll explode. I carefully slide out from under her, gently laying her head on the cushions of the couch. With long, determined strides, I eat up the tiny space between rooms. As I make my way through the cabin, the floorboards creak beneath my feet echoing in the quiet. I cast a glance over to the couch, reassured that she was still asleep, and continue my search for anything usable. I finally come across a dusty duffel bag wedged under the foot of the bed. With a grunt, I drag it out and work the zipper open. Inside is a jackpot. Thumbing through the items, I find flashlights with still-functional batteries, knives, flares, and various tools that could come in handy. My mind quickly calculates their worth and determines my next move. Slinging the bag over my shoulder, I flick on a flashlight.

Keeping the light away from Zoey's peaceful face, I slip out of the cabin. Stepping into the night air, I secure the door with a chain to keep her safe until I return. I slip into the darkness, my movements calculated and silent. An indistinct trail that only my eyes can see, marked with subtle signs that even Zoey didn't notice I made. It guides me deeper into the woods, towards my destination. The spot I took her from. I'm determined to make sure they don't follow us and stop them one way or another. Every rustle in the underbrush sends a jolt of adrenaline through my body as I continue, my senses on high alert. The flashlight illuminates the path in front of me as my feet step into familiar footprints from earlier today. I picture Zoey clopping along behind me in my oversized boots and it makes me even more determined. My heart aches thinking about leaving her alone in that cabin, but I know I have to do this. Hours pass as I walk, my muscles growing tense with each minute that goes by. The faint sound of voices catches my attention.

"Tracks," I hear one voice say.

"On my way," crackles through the walkie-talkie in his hand.

Anger swells up inside of me that I was so careless. Our footprints will lead them right to us. To where I left Zoey sleeping. Alone and defenseless. Flicking off the beam of my flashlight, I creep into position. My feet slide silently through the mud as I creep up behind the man hunched over, studying the boot prints. My heart races with adrenaline as I bring my knife to his throat, dragging it across with precision. He gasps for air, his eyes widening in fear as he struggles against my hold. The metallic scent of blood fills the air, mingling with the earthy aroma of wet soil. I tighten my grip on his mouth and nose, hastening his death. When he finally falls still, I let him drop to the ground. Retrieving the walkie-talkie from the ground next to him, I tuck it into my belt. I admire my work before retrieving the rope from my bag. I twist it around his limp wrists, leaving enough slack for me to drag him along behind me.

The weight of his dead body is heavy as I haul him through the mud, erasing any trace of our presence. Dirt and blood cling to my clothes and skin, but I barely notice as adrenaline courses through my veins. Another obstacle removed. Another mission accomplished. This is the life I have chosen and there is no turning back.

My senses are on high alert as I move through the shadows, my body blending seamlessly with the darkness. Keeping my eyes trained for movement, I ready myself for another kill. My target is the man on the other end of the walkie. Reaching down to my side, I silence the volume and crouch down to wait. Every nerve is taut and ready for action as I scan the area for any signs of movement. I hear his heavy footsteps crunching over the rugged terrain, growing closer and closer before stopping directly in front of me. His gun is slung over his shoulder and his eyes scan the area with a sense of urgency. He has no idea that I am lurking in the darkness or that his partner lies dead at my feet. My grip tightens on my knife. With one swift movement, I lunge forward and wrap my arms around his neck from behind. Startled, he struggles against me, but I hold on tightly, cutting off his air supply. He reaches for his gun but it's too late. With one final twist of my knife, he falls to the ground at my feet. Blood seeps from the wound in his neck as I stand over him, panting heavily.

I quickly search their bodies for any weapons that could be useful before dragging them both deeper into the shadows and hiding them among the trees. With their bodies disposed of and no other signs of life nearby, I gather my things and disappear into the darkness. My mind is already planning my next move as my feet carry me toward my next destination.

As I approach, I slow down and carefully survey the area. My eyes scan for any signs of traps. Finding none, I release a sigh of relief and make my way to a large tree. I climb up, using branches as footholds until I reach a sturdy branch that overlooks the compound. From here, I have a clear view of its layout, more detailed than I originally had from my surveillance on the outskirts.

I study the grounds below me, focusing on the cluster of mid-sized wooden buildings that surround an elaborate, two-story home. It stands tall in the center, elevated above the rest. Its wraparound porch is embellished with hand carved railings running up the steps. From its large windows spills warm light, accentuated by overflowing flower boxes and potted plants that dot the porch and steps. The intricate details of the home make it seem almost alive and welcoming, not like the prison I know it to be. The one where Zoey has been held hostage for years. The thought of her being hidden away, forced to live a lie sends a fiery surge through my veins. She doesn't realize the danger she's in if anyone finds out about her true identity. She's a precious secret and it's my job now to keep her safe.

I lower myself to the ground and slip into the compound undetected. The night air is tense and still, but I move with quiet confidence. Dropping the bag to the ground with a soft thud, I quickly retrieve the flare gun and load it. Taking careful aim, I fire toward one of the surrounding buildings, the bright red flare whizzing through the air before embedding itself into the wall. A thundering boom echoes through the night, followed by frenzied voices and hurried footsteps. As planned, chaos erupts as everyone rushes towards the source of the explosion.

On the front steps of the center house stands the leader of the compound, Zoey's father and a man known for his ruthless tactics. The fury in his voice bellows above the confusion, demanding answers for which his men have none. I reach for my gun where it rests at my side. Taking him out would be a major blow to their operations but it's not the mission. I swallow back the blood lust and focus on what I came here to do. He stomps down the stairs, leaving his sanctuary unattended. My steps are silent as I approach the main building. Blending into the darkness as I slip through the door. I pause and listen for any signs of movement inside but there are no voices or footsteps. Cautiously, I climb the stairs two at a time toward the second floor.

I navigate through a maze of rooms and corridors until I finally reach a bedroom at the end of the hallway. Zoey's room. I know before I even step inside, her presence pulling me.

Her delicate perfume hangs in the air, instantly calming my racing heart. I take a deep breath, savoring every note of her intoxicating fragrance. I work quickly, yanking clothes from hangers and stuffing them into the bag. Bending low to the closet floor, I grab a pair of sneakers and boots. As I stand up to move to the dresser, I catch a glimpse of myself in the mirror and pause. My face is streaked with mud, but it does little to hide the burns and scars that mark my skin. The blood of the men I killed stains me like a permanent reminder of my sins. I am a monster, unworthy of someone as pure and innocent as Zoey. Guilt weighs heavily on my heart as I continue to pack her things, knowing she deserves someone better than me.

Unable to look at myself in the mirror for another second, I tear my eyes away and rummage through her dresser drawers. My hands frantically grab everything I can and shove them into the bag. As my fingers brush against the soft fabric, I pause to look at what I found. I picture the silky thong in my hand hanging on her hips. A jolt of heat shoots through my body and my cock tightens against the zipper of my jeans. Memories flood my mind of the last time I had her panties in my hands. With a twisted grin playing on my lips, I drop the delicate fabric into the bag along with others. I can't think about her like this, especially not now but I can't stop myself. The thought of her innocent smile and the seductive curves of her body consumes me. I shake my head to clear the distracting thoughts from my mind and continue packing. I don't have a lot of time.

Quickly, I move to her nightstand and swipe the books and personal belongings into the bag when something catches my eye. A framed photo of Zoey as a young child and a woman who I assume is her mother. The woman's eyes are clouded with secrets as the two smile at the camera with their arms wrapped around each other's shoulders. I carefully set the photo in the bag and zip it closed.

The sound of heavy footsteps echoes up the stairs, signaling that my time here is running out. I open the window and shimmy over the narrow ledge and down the side disappearing into the darkness where Zoey will be lost to him forever.

Chapter 10
Zoey

The tension I feel when I wake up to find Backdraft no longer next to me is so thick I can barely breathe. The empty space where he should be feels like a gaping void as if he has taken a piece of me with him when he slipped away. What is it about him that stirs such a primal need in me to have him close?

It's irrational, but I jolt from the couch anyway. My feet scramble underneath me as I frantically search for him. The familiar feeling in the pit of my stomach from last night gnaws at my gut.

Is he gone? Did he leave me here?

People leave. They always do. Like the only person I ever truly loved. Memories of my mother flood my mind but they're not the happy ones. Those are tucked back in the farthest corners darkened by the last one I have. The one that haunts me.

Through the tears in my eyes, I can still see her lifeless body swaying from the rafters of our loft. The rope that took her life was drawn so tight around her neck that her flesh was red and raw. Her eyes, once full of life, stared at me with a cold emptiness. That moment is etched into my mind forever. It's the one that makes me push everyone away to protect myself from ever feeling that pain again. Except for Backdraft. He's pushed through so easily, that I can't explain it. It's like he's become a part of me and it's terrifying.

I've been stuck on my father's compound ever since my mom's suicide. At first, I thought he was trying to protect me. 'The world is a cruel place,' he'd tell me. Everything he did was for me. I believed him back then, because at eleven years old, who wouldn't look to their father, their last living relative, to ease the pain? He lost her that night too. Although I never saw him carry the same pain I did or heard his tears late at night. I wanted to believe he kept his emotions hidden to protect me. After a decade though, I realized that he wasn't hiding his emotions to protect me, he simply didn't have any. Not when it came to her and certainly not when it came to me. My home had become a prison. I felt trapped and couldn't breathe. We didn't live off the grid to protect me from men like Backdraft, we lived like that to protect him and his crimes.

I'm lost in my past, drowning in the memory when a jarring sound pulls me back to reality. A loud bang reverberates through the air, causing my heart to race. I fling open the door of the cabin and step out into the bright morning sunshine. My eyes immediately start scanning the area for the source of the noise when they land on Backdraft, bent over the open hood of the truck, his muscular arms flexing as he works on something inside. A torrent of obscenities pours from his lips as he repeatedly slams a hammer against the metal frame. The loud clanging of metal against metal echoes across the clearing, sending a small flock of birds erupting from the treetops.

I catch my breath, my heart thumping in my chest. "Damn it, Backdraft. You scared the life out of me."

Clutching the hammer in his hand, he throws a glare over the hood of the truck, his dark eyes smoldering beneath the shadow of his furrowed brow. My heart does another flop as I watch him work. If you can call it that. Despite his methods, I'm grateful he's with me. I don't know what I was thinking before, I would have never made it this far without him.

"I have that effect on people," he growls, dipping back below the hood of the truck and taking another swing with the hammer. His broad shoulders flex with each strike, veins popping on his biceps from exertion.

"Any luck or are you just playing whack-a-mole with the engine?" I tease, leaning against the truck's faded green bumper. My voice is laced with mock innocence, but my eyes hold a challenge. He challenges me. Makes me feel like the first time in forever I can be myself. I'm not exactly sure who that is but I don't have to guard my words in fear of pissing him off. Although I got a glimpse of him pissed last night and it only added to the heat that radiates off him. He's sexy as all hell and he doesn't even know it.

"Funny girl," he shoots back, sarcasm dripping like the oil from the leaky gasket. "I'm trying to get it started."

"Could've fooled me." I smirk, tilting my head to one side as I watch him tinker with the engine. "Have you considered sweet-talking her? The caveman routine doesn't work on everyone."

Backdraft straightens up, wiping his greasy hands on his jeans. A reluctant smile twitches at the corner of his mouth, betraying his annoyance. "Is that so?"

"Some girls need a gentle touch and a bit of finesse."

"What about you, Little Lamb?" He moves quickly, pinning me against the hood of the truck. His deep voice rumbles through me, causing a surge of desire to wash over me. I swallow hard at the lump forming in my throat when he leans in closer. Every inch of his body is pressed against mine. He's so close I can feel the bulge in his pants. The sheer heat emanating from him shoots a tingling sensation throughout my body. "Do you need finessing or do you like it rough?"

The scent of sweat clings to him, mixing with his natural musky essence. His overwhelming presence stirs a primal urge within me, one that I've never felt before but can't deny. My eyes trace the intricate designs of tattoos that trail up his bulging muscles and onto his chest.

"Maybe you're onto something with the brute force approach," I say, holding onto his gaze. He studies me for a moment. His eyes linger on mine and I feel the air between us shift with an undeniable charge.

"Maybe I am." The tension cracks as he grins at me.

Our banter is a dangerous game, each quip drawing us closer. I rise to my tiptoes trying to bring myself to his level, unable to resist the heat simmering between us. Our breaths mingle, surging with electricity. I wonder what he tastes like.

"You're playing with fire, Little Lamb." My tongue darts out, gently grazing over my parched lips as anticipation builds in my chest. His warm breath fanning against my face, and for a moment, I think he's leaning in for a kiss. I can feel the tension building between us, but instead, frustration creases his features. His brow furrows and those inviting lips tighten into a thin line. A knot forms in my stomach, and I wonder what's holding him back. Is it fear? Uncertainty? Or something else entirely? "I'd hate to see you burn."

He lets out a heavy breath as he pulls away from me. His calloused hands are slick with grease as he runs them through his thick, dark hair. He tugs at the ends in frustration before picking up the hammer and delivering a jolting whack to the engine. My heart jumps out of my chest, my ass ricocheting off the bumper as the metallic clang resonates through me, filling the air between us with tension.

Swirling gray clouds darken the sky suddenly as if the sun has been extinguished along with the moment we shared. Distant thunder growls in warning. The first raindrops hit the ground like scattered bullets, soon followed by a barrage that turns the earth to mud beneath our feet. My heart races, less from the storm and more from the sinking realization that we're stuck.

"Backdraft!" I shout over the wind that rushes in. "We need to get inside!"

He's already on the move, reaching out and grabbing me by the wrist. He pulls me with him, my breath stolen by the fury of the gale that seems hellbent on keeping us right where we don't want to be.

Once inside, Backdraft slams the door against the onslaught of wind and rain barricading it closed with a chair tucked under the handle. The sound of the storm transforms from a roar to a relentless drumming against the roof. It's pitch black until he strikes a match, illuminating his face for a fleeting second before he lights the fire. His eyes meet mine, reflecting a storm of another kind, one that's been brewing between us since we met.

"Cozy," I say, trying to infuse some levity into the situation as I wring out my hair.

"Looks like we're not going anywhere for a while," he grunts. "Should see if there's anything to eat around here before we starve to death."

"I'll do it. You keep the fire going." In the dim light, I rummage through the kitchen, finding cans of Spam and baked beans. Not exactly a feast, but it'll keep the hunger already clawing in my stomach at bay. "Chef Zoey at your service."

Backdraft takes the cans from me and sets them near the growing flames while I return to the kitchen. A brief minute later, I return with two open beers and hand him one.

"I could get used to this," Backdraft says. That smirk that sends my heart hammering in my chest tugs at the corner of his mouth.

I shoot back with a wink and settle onto the floor next to him. Suddenly aware of how the heat from the flames wrap around me even while a chill runs over my arms. The fire crackles and pops, casting a warm glow over the rundown cabin.

"Thanks for the fire," I say softly, handing him a plate.

"Thanks for the grub," he replies, his voice low and laced with a humor that softens the somber feeling in the room.

We eat in silence while the storm outside rages on. It feels almost normal. Like two people sharing a meal rather than two strangers running from danger. As I take small, delicate bites of my meal, I can't help but steal glances at Backdraft. He devours his food with a wild, primal hunger, like a caveman savoring the kill. Each bite is punctuated with a satisfied grunt. His strong jawline and full lips glisten with the remnants of his meal. Although his mannerisms may be uncivilized, it adds to his crude charms and makes me wonder who this man really is. Where did he grow up? Does he have anybody waiting for him at home? I know he mentioned his brothers from his motorcycle club but besides them, whoever they are, is there somebody else?

He catches me staring and wipes his mouth with the back of his hand. He narrows his eyes on me, his gaze hot and slightly intimidating, rendering me completely at his mercy. "What?"

"Nothing." I shrug my shoulders, squirming in my spot while his gaze lingers on me longer than necessary.

"If you have something to say, spit it out."

"When your club finds us or we get out of here, whichever comes first," I wave my hand in the air feigning indifference, "are you going to leave?"

"Hell yeah." He blurts out his unfiltered response with raw honesty and my heart drops to my stomach. I don't know why his answer affects me this much. What did I think, that whatever this is between us means something? Maybe he's right. My innocence is showing through and I hate that. "But I'm taking you with me."

"You are?" My voice cracks. I catch a glimpse of something softer in his eyes, but he quickly masks it with a scowl as he adjusts a log in the fire.

"I'm not leaving you here. I was paid to do a job and that job isn't done until I get you back to Atlantic City."

Reality rams into me head-on like a charging bull. I've been blind, thinking I mean anything more to him than a paycheck. I'm so damn naive.

"Right." I nod acknowledging the full gravity of the situation and stand with a huff, snatching the plastic plate from the floor in front of him.

I toss the dishes into the sink as his heavy steps thunder behind me matching the turbulent storm pelting against the windowpane. I can feel his eyes on me, the heat from his stare boring into my back. I try to ignore him, filling the sink with soap and cold water but his strong hand grabs my shoulder and whirls me around to face him. His dark eyes bleed with anger, trapping me between his hard body and the counter.

His fingers grip my chin, forcing me to look at him, "I didn't mean it like that."

"It's fine," I whisper. "I'm nothing but a job."

I swat at his hand, breaking the contact, and shove him back. I can't deny the sadness that sweeps over me when he steps back, letting me pass.

I leave him standing there and move back toward the fire, suddenly feeling an icy chill so deep in my bones it hurts. As I do, I trip over a duffel bag I didn't notice before.

How long has that been there?

"What's with the bag, Backdraft?"

"Umm," he grunts, "I got you some things."

"What do you mean 'got me some things'?" I ask, parroting his words.

"You have no fucking shoes," he roars. With the side of his boot, he pushes the bag toward me. "You needed some things, so I got you your things."

"My things? You went back there?" I snap, anger flaring as I imagine the risks he took. "Are you insane?"

"It's no big deal."

I'm stunned speechless by his response. Of course, it's a big deal. It's a damn big deal. He could have been killed. I reach for the bag, unzipping it. The first thing I grab is the soft fabric of my favorite shirt, followed by the worn-in sneakers I thought I'd never wear again. As I dig deeper, my fingers brush against the spine of a book. Tears sting my eyes at the thoughtfulness that he went into getting these for me while I am being a complete ass thinking I don't mean a thing to him. Then, like a punch to the gut, I find the small, framed picture of me and my mother. My breath hitches in my throat.

"Backdraft..." I draw the frame out and clutch it to my chest. "You did this for me? Why?"

"Thought you might want your things." I catch a flicker of tenderness in his eyes before he masks it.

"Thank you," I whisper. "But if they caught you..."

"Wouldn't be the first tight spot I've gotten out of." He shrugs, trying to downplay his actions.

I stand up, letting my feet carry me closer to him. As I approach, he opens his arms and pulls me into his chest. His arms wrap tightly around my shoulders, drawing me closer. That familiar heat surges between us. I tilt my face up, locking my teary eyes on his. Every fiber of my being wants him to bridge the gap, to claim my lips with his own. His rough, scarred hand gently traces the curve of my cheek and I lean into his touch, savoring the warmth and tenderness in his calloused fingertips. I can see the torment in his eyes and I want nothing more than to ease the pain he's carrying. He braces himself for me to pull away, but I can't resist the magnetic pull of his touch. "Dax."

Chapter 11
Backdraft

My given name slips through her parted lips in a soft whisper. It's been years since anyone has uttered that name, and the way it sounds on her tongue is both pure and torturous. An unwanted reminder of who I used to be.

My body aches with the intense heat radiating from her and my hard cock twitches in response. The mere thought of touching her sends shivers down my spine. She has no idea how bad I want her, every inch of her flawless skin taunting me. My cock has been throbbing since the moment I laid eyes on her, and it's becoming increasingly difficult to resist the temptation. The fire in her gaze draws me closer, but it's when my eyes drop to her luscious lips that I'm consumed by an insatiable hunger to taste her. Leaning in, our lips hover only inches apart. Her warm breath dances across my mouth, begging me to give in to my desires. With each touch, she ignites a raging inferno inside me, but I know if I succumb to my urges, it will leave us both a smoldering pile of ash.

"I can't touch you, Little Lamb." My jaw clenches with a restraint that borders on pain. "There's enough blood on my hands to bathe the devil and you're an angel I can't tarnish."

"I'm not scared of you." Her delicate fingers curl around the hem of her shirt, slowly lifting it to reveal the smooth expanse of her soft skin. "I want you."

Every inch exposed is an invitation that teases and draws me in. Her movement is slow and seductive, intensifying the struggle within me, making it increasingly difficult to resist reaching out and touching her. My heart races, pounding against my ribcage with a desperate urgency, but I know I have to fight the overwhelming urge no matter how excruciating it feels.

"You should be." I reach out and cover her hands with mine, guiding them back down. "I'm a monster, Little Lamb. I'm a murderer. You've seen it with your own eyes."

She pulls away at the shock of my confession and my heart sinks in my chest. I don't know why I expected anything else. She watched me gun down members of her own family. I wasn't telling her anything she didn't already know.

"Who else have you killed?"

"What? You want me to give you names?" I'm taken aback by her question. She should run away, yet she's standing there with that warm fire blaring in her eyes.

"Tell me. If you're using it as an excuse, then lay it out there. Tell me, Dax. Who else have you killed?"

There's that name again. I grit my teeth. She has no idea she's prodding at the beast that lurks under the surface.

"My father." The words roar out of my mouth dredging up that long-suppressed rage with it. "You want to know more, Little Lamb?"

I stalk toward her, my boots pounding hard on the worn floorboards of the cabin as she steps backward, bumping her ass against the back of the couch. "I lit him on fire and watched as he burned alive."

Then I see it, the fear I need her to feel towards me swallows her whole. Her eyes widen, glistening with tears as she processes my darkest secret. I'm a fucking Bastard, but it's for the best. It's my job to keep her safe until I can get her back to New Jersey. Touching her will only complicate an already bad situation. I can't afford the distraction, not when her father's men are close to picking up on our location.

I grip her wrist in my fist and drag her from the couch. "Time to go."

"We can't leave." She pulls at me, trying to free herself from my grip. "It's not safe out there."

"It's not safe here." I pick up the bag from the floor and toss it over my other arm while tugging her toward the door. My foot kicks at the chair, sending it splintering against the wall, and I yank the door open. All that remains of the storm outside is wet earth and downed trees. The destruction matching the storm she's stirring inside of me.

"Dax, you're hurting me." I grip tighter, no doubt bruising her delicate skin. She doesn't deserve this reaction, but I can't stop it. I let the monster out and now I can't shove him back inside his cage.

Whirling her around, I slam her against the side of the truck. My face is so close to hers that I could give in and claim her lips, feast on her until I'm satiated. Her eyes stare up at me, fear and desire swirling in them. Her lips slightly parted. I lean in closer, drawing those luscious pouty lips between my teeth. I nip so hard I can taste the sweet tang of blood drip onto my tongue. Even when she flinches and lets out a yelp, I don't stop. She pushed me too far and now we're both going to burn.

I couldn't accept it as truth before, but whatever this is between us, I can't deny it anymore. I need her, and like the bastard I am, I take it. I pull her into me and press my lips to hers, claiming her innocence, dragging the sweet angel in front of me down into the fiery pits of hell where I live. I kiss her furiously until the voices in my head are silent and the most satisfying moan rips from her throat.

She will hate me after this, but I don't care. I have to have her. The swelling need inside of me is at odds with the reality of the situation. I can't keep her. She's not mine. We're from two different worlds and someone is waiting for her back in New Jersey where I'm supposed to deliver her. I don't know how I'll give her up after this, but I know I'll have to. That reality guts me deeply.

A bang in the distance rips a sharp breath from my lungs.

"Get in the truck." I pull the passenger side door open.

Zoey nods once, slipping into the old pickup truck and I close her in. I dart around to the other side and slide onto the cracked leather seat next to her. Maneuvering my hands below the steering wheel, I pry off the cover and fiddle with the wires. After a few tries, I connect the right two, making the truck's headlights flicker on and the engine click.

Sucking in a deep breath, I jump out of the truck and run to the front to pop the hood. Spotting the hammer that I left on the ground earlier, I pick it up and bring it down in a hard strike against the starter. After the third hit, the engine finally turns over. I let out a sigh of relief and slam the hood down before climbing back into the driver's seat. I toss the hammer onto the cluttered floorboard behind the seat. I shift into drive and give the gas pedal gentle taps. The engine sputters and jerks after sitting idle for so long, but with a little finesse, I coax the heap of junk into moving forward. Pressing the accelerator further to the floor, I will the truck to go faster. It lurches forward, throwing up a cloud of smoke as I speed down the muddy trail.

"Hold on tight."

Zoey clenches the door handle, her knuckles turning white from holding on so tight as we take off down the mountain road. My fingers curl around the steering wheel as the old truck rumbles away from the security of the cabin. We wind our way through the trees, the branches whipping past the windows like angry fingers trying to pull us back. Zoey shifts in the seat beside me, her knee brushing my thigh. Even the most subtle contact shoots sparks through every part of me.

I shift in my seat, trying to ease the ache in my cock. But moving only makes it worse, grinding my erection against the rough denim of my jeans. I risk a glance at her, taking in the soft curve of her cheek, the way the sunlight kisses her hair with gold. My chest tightens. A maelstrom of conflicting emotions races through my mind. Being close to her is sweet agony.

She's good and pure, and I'm anything but. Kissing her was wrong. I need to keep my distance for both our sakes, but I know I won't be able to bring myself to do it.

Silence lingers between us, broken only by the churn of gravel under the truck's tires when I emerge from the dirt trail onto a more promising route.

***

The road stretches endlessly through the thick woods. We drive for hours, winding back and forth, descending one mountain to climb another. I have no damn idea where we are or where to go next, but with Zoey safe next to me, I keep driving even as the sun begins to set beyond the treetops. I can't risk stopping.

Zoey's hand comes to rest on my thigh. I swallow hard, keeping my eyes fixed on the road. Her hand stills on my leg, her warmth seeping through my pants. After a long moment, Zoey yawns and leans back in her seat, withdrawing her hand and drawing my eyes along with it. I'm helpless to resist her, and that scares the hell out of me.

"Watch out!" Zoey yells and darts up in her seat.

I jerk my head back toward the road and spot the deer running in front of me. My foot instinctively slams on the brake. The tires screech in protest and the truck lurches forward, losing traction and fishtailing half off the road as it skids to a stop a few inches from colliding with a tree.

"Shit." My heart is pounding, and I exhale the breath I was holding. "Are you OK?"

"I think so."

Shifting the truck into park, I reconnect the wires that broke loose but the engine only gives a dull click in response.

"Stay here."

I step out of the truck and lift the hood. A cloud of steam billows out. Cursing under my breath, knowing damn well this piece of shit overheated and the starter died again from the sudden stop and the strain of the drive. With gritted teeth, I let out a loud growl and give the truck a swift kick. The sound of my steel toed boot meeting metal echoes through the deserted woods as if mocking me. Stalking around to the side, my eyes sweep over the muddy truck and the area surrounding it. Trees and shrubs. Dirt and rocks. Nothing but the same old shit stretches out before me with no sign of civilization in sight. The sun is slipping further behind the mountains and soon we'll be stranded in complete darkness. The crunch of gravel under my feet only adds to my irritation.

What is wrong with me? I'm trained to handle situations like this, to remain detached and professional. Yet around her, I feel like I've lost my fucking mind. Nothing about this assignment has gone right. I need a minute to think.

I shove my hands in the pockets of my pants. My fingers curl around the silky fabric wedged in the creases. Withdrawing my hand, I stare down at her panties I forgot I had.

"Dax?" My name on her lips shatters my control.

Spinning around again, I catch her amber eyes glowing like flames in the dark. I trek towards her. Each step falls heavier than the last as I close the distance between us, pinning her against the rear of the truck. With her panties still in my hands, my fingers encircle her throat. Not tight enough to constrict her breathing but just enough that her body jerks taut.

I hate how I react to the sound of my name, even when it comes out of her perfect fuckable mouth. "Don't call me that."

"Why? It's your name and I like it." Her voice quivers when she says it again, pushing me further past my breaking point. "Dax."

"It's Backdraft. Haven't been anyone else in a long time." My voice lowers, my eyes dropping to her lips.

I kiss her, hungry and desperate, pouring all my frustrations into her. She responds without hesitation, meeting me need for need. Her mouth molding to mine is a perfect fit. Slightly pulling back, I loosen my grip on her neck and search her eyes. She's not afraid in the least. She's staring up at me with needy eyes that make my cock throb. Her hand slides under my shirt, her touch like a brand against my scarred skin. Her fingers trace the edges of my scars.

"You're a good man, Backdraft, and I want you. Scars and all."

The fierce conviction in her voice cracks my resistance. I crush her to me, claiming her mouth again as my hands roam over her body. There is no turning back. Now that I've had a taste of her, I need more.

"Be careful what you ask for, Little Lamb." My deep voice rumbles in my chest, vibrating against her and sending goosebumps down her arms.

I draw my rough hands down her arms, soothing the chill. She lets out a soft moan and I slide my hand behind her back. In one swift move, I spin her around. I don't fuck face-to-face. I don't like having eyes on me when I get off. The scars and burns that make me look dangerous cover most of my body. She might find them dangerous now, but that thrill will run its course. It always does.

Her front is pressed against the side of the truck, my hardness pushing against her ass. My heart races in my chest. I know it's not fair, but I can't stop it. I've lost all control, and I need her more than I've ever needed anyone.

I yank at the sweatpants hanging off her hips until her bare ass is displayed before me. "Fucking hell woman. Do you know what you do to me?"

"Show me." She's all but begging me to take her and I can't refuse her pleas anymore.

My hand strokes her leg, sliding up her inner thigh. She moans and it sounds so damn sexy I almost jizz in my pants. Using my feet, I spread her legs wider letting my fingers roam higher until they reach the wetness between her legs. My thumb rubs against her clit and she releases a breath in a sharp pant that only makes me want her more. I slide my finger inside her sweet pussy, and she jerks forward, her hands clinging to the side of the truck.

"Is this what you want, Little Lamb?" She rocks back against me, her body needy and demanding.

She's so fucking wet for me, I can hardly think straight. I yank at the button of my jeans and draw the zipper down. Working them over my hips, I free my hard cock from its confines. My erection presses against the swell of her ass.

"Yes," she purrs. "I want you."

Gripping my hands on her hips, I line myself up and push inside. No foreplay, no easing her into it. I'm a fucking Bastard and I know it. She gasps when I enter her, her fingers gripping tighter to the edge of the truck. She feels so fucking perfect. I push deeper, sheathing my full length in her welcoming heat. For the first time in my life, I feel whole. With Zoey, I'm not broken or scarred. I'm just a man, giving myself to a woman who wants me.

"Remember, you asked for this, Little Lamb."

Her head falls forward and her breath quickens as she moans for me. My hand roams up her spine, arched perfectly into me until I reach the nape of her neck. Fisting her hair, I tug her head back bringing her closer and nip at her neck. I suck her soft flesh between my teeth, marking her.

"You make me so fucking crazy."

With hard deep thrusts, I fuck her mercilessly until her thighs shake and her pussy pulses around me. My balls seize up and jerk taut, making me quickly pull out of her heat. My hands close around her panties and I cover the head of my cock like I did before, exploding thick hot torrents into the silky fabric.

Releasing my satiated dick, I watch as the shockwaves continue to rack her body. I roll her onto her back, the scent of sweat mixing with her sweet aroma. I look down at her, her body shaking in my grasp as our breathing slowly returns to normal. I brush a strand of hair away from her face, my fingers lingering on her soft skin. She opens her eyes and looks up at me with a mix of pleasure and vulnerability. My mind is still reeling from what I just did. I let my desire and need consume me and now I feel like an asshole.

A warm, rosy blush spreads across her cheeks, as her gaze flickers between me and her panties. "I was wondering what happened to those."

A small smile plays on her lips as she waits for my response. With a dismissive shrug, I fling the panties into the back of the truck. As she pulls the oversized sweatpants up to cover herself, I tuck myself into my jeans.

"It's too dark to work on the truck. Get in, we'll be sleeping here tonight."

Chapter 12
Zoey

It wasn't the way I pictured my first time but the way he ravaged my body was all-consuming. Every inch of me was overtaken by his touch, leaving no space for thought or doubt. I spent most of my life desperate for affection, needing to be loved, and in that moment with his hands on me, it was enough. They were rough and urgent, yet they conveyed everything he couldn't say. He may not believe he's worthy of love, but I know he's wrong. It's in the way he looks at me, with adoration and protectiveness. He may not express it in traditional ways, but his touch speaks louder than words ever could.

As I climb back into the safety of the truck, I can still feel him inside me, filling every inch of me. It was raw, passionate and beautiful.

Backdraft cranks my window down a crack, pushes the manual lock down, and secures me inside. After a few long minutes, the hood of the truck slams closed. The thud in the quiet night makes me jump, but I ease back into the seat when his eyes meet mine for a split second. I don't miss the way he averts his gaze and circles around to the other side of the truck. He slides into the driver's seat, doing the same to his window and door. We sit in silence, only the rapid beating of my heart breaking up the quiet.

I can't stop replaying the feel of his lips on mine, the way my heart raced when he touched me. I'd never felt so alive, so wanted, and I'm already missing that feeling. I steal a glance in his direction. His eyes are fixed on the darkness creeping in through the windows.

Backdraft doesn't strike me as a man who startles. He has nerves of steel and body to match but right now he's more on edge than I've ever seen him. I don't know if it's the situation we find ourselves stuck in or what happened between us. Something shifted back there, we both felt it. There's no denying the obvious connection but he's already told me he doesn't plan on staying. I'm a job to him. I should hate him for that. I should hate myself for falling so easily for him. But I don't. I don't regret a moment of what we shared. I'd give myself to him all over again to feel like that one more time.

The darkness has crept in, blanketing us in an eerie silence. The only light is from the lightning bugs, flashing and flickering in perfect rhythm. I look to the front window, knowing that this will be over soon, and when it is, Backdraft will be gone. The problem is, I don't know how I'll ever return to my old life. A life without him in it. The weight of this truth hits me hard and I slump into my seat.

I'm the first to speak, hoping to break the tension. "They're beautiful, aren't they?"

Next to me, Backdraft grunts and shrugs his shoulders, masking any emotions behind his tough exterior while digging through the duffel bag. Pulling out a flashlight, he flips it on and sets it on the seat between us. Then he hands me my sneakers before tossing the bag back on the floorboard behind our seat.

He looks at me then with his deep gray eyes. Butterflies flip and twirl in my belly.

"Come here." He tips his head to where he wants me.

I swallow hard, every nerve in my body tingling in anticipation. I can see he's already hard and I'm not even touching him yet. I love that I can do that to him. Shifting in the seat, I turn to straddle him.

"Turn around, Little Lamb, keep your eyes on the outside."

Although confused, I do what he asks and swing my leg over to climb onto his lap.

His hardness presses against my ass and my body clenches in response.

"Are you sore?" he asks, gently caressing the ache between my legs through my pants. I can already feel myself getting wet from the warmth of his hand.

"Yes," I answer quietly, slightly embarrassed. I'm sore as hell but I don't want my inexperience to disappoint him. "A little."

"I'm sorry I used you like that, Little Lamb. You didn't deserve that."

I reach back, stroking the stubble on his face with my fingertips. "You didn't use me, Backdraft. I wanted it and I enjoyed it."

The light is dim making it hard to see his expression, but I think he's grinning.

He leans forward, his lips on the curve of my neck, and whispers, "Let me make it up to you."

My heart races when his hand slides under my pants and his palm grazes my bare skin. My breath catches in my throat as his fingertips glide over my swollen nub. He rolls them in small circles sending a wave of ecstasy through my entire body. I begin to rock back and forth as he slides his fingers into me. He's taking his time, caressing and teasing in deep but gentle strokes. Every nerve in my body is alive and tingling from his touch. My thighs shake from the building pressure, and for a moment, I forget where we are. All I can focus on is the tidal wave washing over me.

"That's it, Little Lamb. Come on my fingers."

My release hits me hard. My core tightens around his fingers. I cry out, a rushed moan ripping from my lips. His fingers continue to pump inside of me as I roll into them, riding my orgasm for as long as I can. I collapse forward onto the steering wheel, gasping for air. He eases his fingers out of me while I catch my breath.

This man has me twisted in knots and I can't figure him out. It's like there's two sides to him. One that is dark and commanding while the other is tender. One who ravishes me like a wild animal and one whose sole focus is on pleasing me. Somehow, they coexist, creating an electrifying and irresistible combination that keeps me wanting more.

"Backdraft?" I ask, being careful to use his road name since his real name, Dax, seems to elicit something dark and primal inside of him.

"Yes, Little Lamb?" His voice rumbles low and gravelly, sending shivers down my spine.

"Why do you call me that?" My heart races as his hand trails down my neck, leaving a trail of heat in its wake.

His fingers tangle in the long strands of my hair, pulling it back to expose my vulnerable neck. "Because you appear innocent and sweet on the surface, but when pushed into a corner, you're fierce."

With a predatory smile, he shifts me off his lap onto the seat next to him. "We're in for a long night. Get some sleep."

I try to resist, but my eyes are heavy, and my mind is hazy from the mind-blowing orgasms. Giving in to exhaustion, I rest my head on his lap. I succumb to the peaceful rhythm of his breathing, feeling completely content, and fall asleep.

Chapter 13
Backdraft

Shortly after Zoey drifted to sleep, I turned the flashlight off, plunging us deeper into the darkness. I sat there, her body tangled against mine as my eyes swept between her and any potential danger outside.

I couldn't sleep, not with Zoey curled against me. Her warmth seeps through my pants and straight to my cock. My body is acutely aware of every point of contact, from the press of her breasts against my leg to the slide of her thigh under my arm. When she made those soft whimpers and nuzzled even closer, I nearly lost my mind. Torn between waking her just so I can touch her again and keeping a lookout, it took all the self-control I could muster to let her sleep.

Disoriented, I strain my eyes to watch the sun slowly peek over the jagged hilltops, casting a warm orange glow on the surrounding trees. My vision is hazy and unfocused, but I make out a faint glimpse of civilization in the distance. It was already dark when we broke down, so I couldn't see it. But now, in the light of day, it becomes clear. A small town nestled in a valley between the rolling hills, not too far away. The glimmer of sunlight against the rooftops of the clustered buildings is a welcome sight after all this time spent in the wilderness. My tired body perks up with renewed energy, knowing that safety is within reach at last.

I stretch my stiff muscles and rub the sleep from my own eyes before waking Zoey. Her head is still pillowed on my lap, her long hair fanned out against me. I sweep the loose strands away from her face and she stretches out, shifting away from me. The oversized sweatpants she's still wearing slip down to reveal the top curve of her ass. I quickly look away and adjust myself to hide my morning erection.

Zoey sits up and rubs the sleep from her eyes before taking in the sight for herself. She lets out a relieved sigh, "Is that a town?"

I nod, "Looks like it. Hope we're not walking." The truck has had plenty of time to cool down overnight. I just need to get it running again. I press the frayed wires together and it taunts me with hesitant sputters.

Grabbing the hammer from the back, I hop out of the driver's seat and lift the hood. We've made it this far; this baby will get us the rest of the way whether it wants to or not.

With a swift strike, I bring the hammer down on the faulty starter. The engine turns over, responding with a low growl. With a smug grin on my face, I close the hood and climb back in.

Snatching Zoey by the waist, I drag her to me. Our lips meet in a heated kiss.

Just then my phone starts ringing, breaking us apart. As much as I want to keep kissing her, it's a welcome sound after days without a signal. I fumble it out of my pocket, wincing at the cracks in the screen stopping me from seeing who's calling. Whoever's on the other end better not be a fucking telemarketer. "Yeah?"

Zoey's gaze shifts to mine, and for a brief second, I catch a glimpse of sadness before she schools her features and gives me that sweet smile.

"It's Aero. I've been trying to reach you for days. What the hell happened to you?"

Relief floods through me at the sound of my president's voice. "I've been lost in the fucking wilderness with no signal."

"We've been scouring the area for you since you went dark. Your phone just went back online. Do you have the girl?"

Out of the corner of my eyes, I look at Zoey. I have the girl all right, and when Aero finds out, he will skin my ass alive. Zoey smiles at me, and just like that, I don't give a damn about the consequences. I nod, even though he can't see me. "I do. Looks like a town about a half day's walk, if this heap of metal I found can't make it."

"Good work. Got a lock on your location. Make it to town. The boys and I will be there with backup within the hour."

"Copy that." I end the call.

The truck jerks as I work it back onto the road. Yesterday's storm is now an afterthought as the morning sun already heats the air, drying everything in sight. Dirt and gravel kick up under the tires when I take off in the only direction I can go.

"What are you going to do first?" I ask Zoey. I'm no good at small talk, but if I can't touch her, hearing her voice is the next best thing.

She smiles wide for the first time. "Eat. I'm starving. Bacon and eggs, maybe hotcakes. Oh, and some country biscuits and sausage and gravy." She rubs her rumbling stomach. "What do you want to do?"

I look at her and a grin crawls across my face. It's an odd feeling but I like the effect she has on me. "Shower, shit, eat and fuck you. Not necessarily in that order."

Her laughter fills the truck cabin. It's the most infectious sound I ever heard and suddenly I'm laughing too.

Until I round the bend and find the road blocked by a line of vehicles with heavily armed men taking cover behind them.

"Shit," I hiss, slamming the truck into reverse. Bullets ping off the hood, shattering the windshield. I drag Zoey down onto my lap, shielding her as the truck spins out of control and dies.

"Stay down." I duck down out of the line of fire and reach for my gun. Checking the clip, I reload and aim out of the passenger window now lined up with the firing squad. I aim and fire back.

Zoey trembles on my lap, her terrified cries gutting me. I led her right into the line of fire simply because I had to get out of that cabin. I needed distance between her and the place where I let my deepest secret come out into the light. I can't take the words back, but I can fight like hell to make sure those words aren't what she remembers when she looks at me.

When the shooters pause to reload, I grab Zoey's hand and dive out of the truck, scrambling behind it for cover but we're outnumbered and trapped. Gripping my pistol, I steel myself for the next wave of bullets.

"Give us the girl if you want to walk away from this," someone shouts.

"Don't make me go back." Zoey pleads with me. Hasn't she figured out yet that I'd never let that happen? Not just because I was hired to rescue her from this group of nuts but because she's mine now. It wasn't meant to happen. It shouldn't have happened, but I can't change things now and I wouldn't take it back if I could. Zoey is an angel sent to help me atone for my sins. I never believed in fate or God but how else can I explain the fact that she soothes the fire licking my skin, the need embedded so deep inside of me that makes me want to burn the world to ash?

"You're not going anywhere, Little Lamb."

I pull my side piece from my ankle holder and hold it out to her, "Do you know how to use this?"

She shakes her head, her big doe eyes wide with shock.

"It's easy, Little Lamb. You don't have to kill anyone, just help me keep them back." I pull her in front of me, so her back is flush against my chest and guide the pistol between her hands. Keeping a firm grip on her, I position one arm tight against her body. "Keep this arm tucked in close and aim for your target. Pull the trigger back with your finger. It's small but it has power so be careful. Keep your pretty, little head low.

Don't make yourself a target. Are you ready?"

She nods her head, uncertain but willing to do what it takes. Inhaling a deep breath, I take in the sight of my Little Lamb poised for action. It's hot as fuck.

"Let's do this shit." I signal her and yell back to the man demanding I give her back. Fat chance in hell that will ever happen. "I'll take my chances."

Simultaneously, we return fire pushing them back behind their vehicles. We have to survive long enough for the club to arrive. When Aero notices that my signal has stopped moving and we didn't make it to town, he'll be here. I have to trust in that. Trust my President and my new club even though trust is not my strong suit.

Zoey is holding her own, firing her gun, and taking cover when needed. Her aim isn't as steady as mine, but for a first-timer, I'm impressed with how she's handling herself. I glance over at her as we take a quick break from exchanging fire to reload. She's crouched down behind the truck next to me, loose strands of her hair falling around her face and sticking to the sweat on her forehead, but she looks beautiful.

"Are you doing alright?" I ask, trying to keep the worry out of my voice. I hate that she's been put in this situation when all I want to do is protect her and keep her safe.

She nods without looking at me. "Yeah, I'm good."

There's only enough time to fire off a quick 911 text to Aero before another round of bullets ping off the truck and we're back in action.

We keep up this back-and-forth for what feels like hours until the sound of motorcycle engines fill the air, the rumble shaking the ground beneath us. Relief rushes through me knowing backup has arrived at last.

The sudden attack splits their focus, dividing their attention between us and the roaring motorcycles firing at them from behind. The air is filled with the deafening sound of bullets and revving engines as chaos erupts all around us. I rise and unleash a barrage of gunfire, providing cover for my comrades. Zoey joins me, her aim now steady and deadly.

Aero leads the attack while the familiar faces of my club brothers ride alongside him. Behind them follow more bikers with similar cuts as ours. Executing precise movements, they take control of the situation and together we eliminate our attackers with deadly accuracy. When the gunfire stops, I grab Zoey by the hand, pulling her down behind the truck.

"You did great, Little Lamb."

I thread my fingers through her long hair and draw her close, crushing my lips to hers. She holds herself up with one arm and the other curls around my bicep as I hold her close and devour her mouth with a fierce kiss. The sound of boots crunching gravel interrupts the moment. For a second, I was so lost in her that I almost wished we were still alone and not about to be surrounded by my club.

Taking her by the hand, we join the others. Aero scans us from head to toe, his eyes narrowing in on her fingers woven between mine. I stare at him with wide eyes and feel the tension in the air, but he contains his sneer and doesn't acknowledge the way we're clinging to each other. I give her hand a gentle squeeze before releasing it.

Aero slaps me on the shoulder and pulls me into an unexpected hug. "Good to see you in one piece."

Normally, I wouldn't be so open to this kind of physical contact, but my club came through for me in a big way and I'm realizing just how much this brotherhood means to me. Leaning into it, I pat his back, "Thanks for the assist, Pres."

I turn to Zoey. "Zoey, these are the guys I told you about. My club brothers. Aero is our President. This is Surge, our Sergeant at Arms, Padre is the club Secretary and Crank is our Road Captain." I point each one out to her. Her eyes follow along taking it all in, even though it's a lot to process. "That's Tango the Cleaner, Pike is Tail Gunner, Rancor is the Treasurer, and Hashtag is our Tech guy."

The guys fall into a subtle rhythm of acknowledgment. Some offer handshakes while others give a quick nod or a tip of their heads. I recognize a few faces from the Nashville Chapter as we walk towards them standing by their bikes. We met briefly during my stopover at Royal Road, but it was enough for them to know that I was on their turf and had come to do a job. I'm grateful they showed up to lend a hand. The first one to catch my attention is Thorn, clad in leather. He tops off his look with a sleek cowboy hat. A thick beard hides his face and I can't spot any tattoos on his arms. Next to him is their VP, Pagan. He towers over the group with his large build and bushy beard. With light brown hair peeking out from under his bandana, he gives off a backwoods vibe. Villain's appearance is deceiving. He's a blonde man with clean-cut features. He could easily be mistaken for a Disney prince, but there's an air of darkness about him that makes me wonder if he lives up to his name. And then there's Irish, their Enforcer. He's a fiery redhead with a muscular build and an impressive reputation as an MMA fighter. I tip my head to acknowledge them and they return the gesture.

"Let's get out of here," Aero says, his eyes scanning our surroundings for any potential threats.

"Would love to, but I don't have wheels." I look back at the truck. It was a beater to begin with but now it's riddled with bullet holes and flat tires.

"Got your bike back at Royal Road, man," Thorn informs me.

"Guess you're riding bitch." Surge laughs and I hit him with a side eye.

"Saddle up, big fella. The girl rides with me." Aero leads Zoey to his bike. Fear floods her big brown eyes and locks on mine. I reassure her with a quick smile and a nod that only she catches. Hesitantly, she follows Aero. He straddles his bike and hands her a helmet. With it secure on her head, he reaches out and helps her climb onto the back of his bike. Jealousy grips a hold of me, my back tenses up and my fists clench at my side.

Reaching into the back of the truck, I grab the duffel bag with Zoey's things.

Seeing what they meant to her, it would be a shame to leave them behind. I turn towards my brothers, who are all climbing onto their rides, crowding their seats. Motherfuckers, all of them.

"Looks like Hashtag's prepared for a back warmer." Everyone but Hashtag and I erupt into laughter. Sure, stick me with the smallest guy in the club. I'm surprised he can even hold his bike upright. Adding my weight is a recipe for disaster. Dangling from the back of his bike right above the decal with some witty coding joke no one else gets is a spare helmet with some Matrix code bullshit on it that matches the one plastered to his head.

I'd expect Aero to come prepared with a spare helmet for Zoey. He's the chapter president for a reason. Always one step ahead but Hashtag? I shake my head and reluctantly tread toward him. He's a fucking Boy Scout.

I contemplate walking, but I'm ready to get the hell out of these woods and there's already too much distance between Zoey and me. I grumble out loud and squeeze the small helmet as far on my head as it can fit, tightening the strap under my chin. I cast one more look at Zoey. Once confident she's safe, I wrap the handles of the duffle bag over the sissy bar and climb on the seat behind Hashtag and ride bitch. He tips the bike a little, adjusting to the extra weight but quickly gets the hang of it. With a roar, we all take off in a cloud of dust and gravel.

Chapter 14
Zoey

I tried to avert my gaze, but despite my efforts, something within me compelled me to look. My heart raced as I scanned the faces of the dead bodies scattered across the ground. I had to know if my father was among them. A strange mix of emotions flooded through me, relief he wasn't one of the fallen, yet also a tinge of disappointment. I look closer to be sure and that's when it hits me that Justin isn't here either.

The arrival of Backdraft's club had been a blur of chaos and adrenaline, leaving me wondering if they managed to escape. My heart felt heavy with the uncertainty of it all. Is it truly over now? Will my father finally release his hold on me? As questions buzz through my mind, they all lead back to the single thought weighing heaviest on my mind. What would become of Backdraft and me now?

Even holding tight to Aero's back, I can still smell Backdraft on my clothes. I can feel him on my skin. I can taste him on my lips. We're moving so fast that the wind slaps me in the face, but I cram my neck as far as I can to catch a glimpse of Backdraft. He's riding behind one of the club members with a scowl on his face. I giggle under my breath at the sight. He's donning a helmet that seems to be more for show than actual protection, barely covering the top of his head. He perches awkwardly so far back on the seat that it looks like he has a backrest wedgie lodged where the sun doesn't shine. His arms are stretched behind him, fingers white-knuckled around the backrest. The wind whips through my hair and the exhilarating sensation of speed is all too intoxicating. The thrill is already coursing through my veins, and I can't wait for my turn to ride behind Backdraft instead of Aero.

Had someone told me a week ago that my entire life would be flipped upside down because of one foolish decision, I would have laughed in their face. Yet here I am in the midst of chaos, surrounded by a group of guys whose interactions with each other fills me with a longing that I never knew existed. It's like missing something you never had to begin with. After spending years under the suffocating control of my father and living off the grid with a ragtag clan of extremists, I find myself wanting to be a part of it. The butterflies fluttering in my stomach tell me it's true. They've taken up residency since the moment I first laid eyes on Backdraft. And now, flying down the open road with the wind whipping through my hair, and the tires spinning so fast they blur, those butterflies only intensify. It's a rush unlike anything I've ever experienced before, a perfect combination of danger and freedom that leaves me craving more with every passing mile.

The bikes slow as we approach the old industrial part of the city, flanked on either side by rows of towering warehouses. We continue down the narrow road, weaving through the buildings until eventually pulling through a gate and coming to a complete stop in front of the largest warehouse of them all. The steel giant looms over us, dwarfing these men. The only sound is the low rumble of engines idling. One by one the engines shut off and an eerie feeling washes over me.

"Where are we?" I ask, climbing off Aero's bike in front of a large warehouse.

"This is just a pitstop so you can clean up and rest. In the morning, we'll leave for home." Aero places his hand on my arm. "This must be confusing for you, but it'll all make sense when we get back to Atlantic City. Can you trust us?"

I point to Backdraft. "I trust him."

Aero stares at me for a minute and I swallow hard realizing I stuck my foot in my mouth and insulted the President of the club when he's trying to be nice.

After a beat, Aero nods his head. "Good."

He motions for me to walk in front of him where I find Backdraft heading towards me. The two exchange a look before Backdraft protectively pulls me into his side and Aero continues into the warehouse.

"Listen to me, Little Lamb, this place is going to be a lot to handle. I don't want you wandering around here alone. This club is nothing like ours, so don't get the wrong idea about us."

I don't understand what he means, but nod in acceptance of what he's asking of me. It's not until we step inside that it becomes clear.

Chapter 15
Backdraft

Thorn leads us into Royal Road, and the scene playing out in front of our eyes is the same as it was the last time I was here. Only I'm not the same man. Half-naked women clinging onto any warm body they can attach to, their bodies swaying to the loud music blasting through the halls. The air is thick with the smell of sweat, alcohol, and sex.

"This way." Thorn leads us through the ornately decorated halls of Royal Road to where Kingpin, the Nashville Chapter President, is waiting.

There, in the center of the room, commanding the attention of those around him sits Kingpin on a throne of red velvet. His reputation precedes him. He's shirtless, covered in intricate, black-inked tattoos, wearing nothing but his cut and black leather pants. His long dark hair falls in straight strands, and a full beard frames his jawline. Black mascara lines his lashes and matches the black polish on his hands and tattooed feet. He stands out in the crowd, not fitting the bill of Nashville by a long shot.

"Welcome to Royal Road." Even from across the room, I can feel the way his eyes roam over Zoey. I pull her in closer with a firm grip around her waist, making my position clear. I don't miss the way Aero sneers and grumbles under his breath, but I plan on keeping her close. Our chapters may be part of the same club, but that doesn't mean I have to trust him.

"Looks like you recovered more than just your man." Kingpin's smirk makes me want to knock it off his face, but I know better. His chapter is bigger than ours and I'd have them all on my ass in a New York minute if I tried. And when they were through, Aero would have what's left.

Aero nods, "Appreciate you lending me your men. I got what I came here for."

Kingpin jumps down from his throne. "What about the girl? She's a Cassedy, isn't she?"

Aero steps between us and I appreciate his display of protection. "This is Zoey."

"The Cassedy Clan is a bunch of idiots, but we've done business a time or two. What do you want with Dominic's daughter?"

"That's our club's business, but I will say, she is extremely important to us."

Kingpin's head cocks to the side, ignoring my hold on her. "Are you here willingly?"

My body tenses, unsure how she'll answer. She left with me willingly. Didn't she? She gave herself to me willingly. Didn't she? As if she can sense what I'm thinking, Zoey's grip tightens around my hand. She clears her throat, and answers without an ounce of wavering, her voice loud and her desire clear, "Yes."

I exhale the breath caught in my lungs. Kingpin and Aero lock eyes in a standoff before he concedes and offers a singular nod. "Then she's welcome to stay. I'll have someone show her to a room and then we can discuss business."

"Appreciated." Aero acknowledges him but doesn't back down from his stance between us.

With his arm raised in the air, Kingpin snaps his fingers, and out of nowhere appears a woman. "Follow me, darlin'. I'll show you to a room with a hot shower. I can arrange for some food if you're hungry."

Zoey turns towards me, her amber eyes burning into my soul. "You're not coming with me?"

Draping the duffel bag on her shoulder, I lean in close and lower my voice so only she can hear. "I can't, Little Lamb, but you're safe here. Just remember what I said. Stay in your room until one of us comes to get you."

She nods her head, keeping her eyes lowered away from mine, and doesn't say a word. I wonder if it's because she's afraid her voice will break while fighting back unshed tears. If she looks at me, she'll see that the look of rejection on her face is gutting me to my core. I never want her to feel the way I'm making her feel right now. I want to tell her that there's nothing I want more than to keep her by my side but right now we have business to deal with and it shouldn't be done with her in the room. Besides the fact, I'm still feeling out how Aero will react to us together.

My hand lingers on Zoey's for too long. The last thing I want to do is let her go. I don't know when I'll get to hold her again. Aero clears his throat and the reaction jerks me back to reality with a hard snap. She isn't supposed to be mine. I was only supposed to find her and bring her back to Atlantic City so she could learn the truth about who she was. Someone who's not meant to be with a biker with scars as deep as mine. I let my hand slip from hers and watch as she walks away taking a splinter of my heart with her. Something shifts inside of me and there's no longer any doubt in my mind. She's mine.

When the women are out of the room, the tension eases.

"Is there anything I should know?" Kingpin asks.

"Left a lot of Cassedy's men face down in the dirt," Aero answers curtly with a shrug.

"Not good for my dealings," Kingpin states, pacing back and forth.

"Neither's the fact they were selling explosives to the Asphalt Gods," I speak up. Kingpin and Aero both snap their heads in my direction.

"How do you know this?" Kingpin questions.

"Cause I blew a few up."

"Well, shit." Kingpin erupts into a laugh, patting me on the shoulder. "Enjoy your stay, fellas. Royal Road is the playground of the Royal Bastards and you've been granted admission. Pussy over there," Kingpin swings his arm out wide in one direction and then the other, "gambling over there. Anything else you fancy you can find in these walls too."

"Get some sleep too. We're pulling out in the morning." Aero orders as we all filter out of the throne room and into the massive establishment known as Royal Road. The men's eyes glaze over with lust, drool practically puddling from their mouths thinking about free pussy for the taking. Aero and Surge try to discreetly slip away but it doesn't go unnoticed.

"You're not coming with us?" Crank asks.

"Thought I'd leave some for you," Aero quips. "Gonna hit the tables."

The guys burst into laughter, slapping each other on the back and tapping fists like a punch of adolescent boys at the first encounter of snatch. I'm starting to understand why Surge wouldn't be interested in strippers and club girls. He's the only one of us with an actual Ol' Lady back at the clubhouse. When Emery came to stay, she brought her friend Lacey along. She's taken up residence with us temporarily but seems to be a permanent fixture warming Aero's bed even though he hasn't officially claimed her yet. I wonder if that has more bearing on why he's not indulging in what Kingpin's club has to offer more than the fact that he's our President and still trying to get his bearings and earn our respect. Being a new chapter made up of nomads, we're all still finding our footing. We may not have known each other as long as the members of other chapters or be as big as this one, but we've connected instantly and I have no doubt we all take our newfound brotherhood seriously. Regardless of his reasons, I'm right there with Aero and Surge. The thought of those women are not affecting my cock whatsoever. There's only one woman my cock is responding to and I slip away silently in search of her.

Chapter 16
Zoey

I should be used to being alone. I've spent most of my life that way, but since Backdraft came into my life, the feeling is heart wrenching. I've been there. I've done that. And I never want to do it again. Yet here I am. Alone. I don't know what it is keeping Backdraft away, but I know he wants me even if he's struggling with it. I've seen the way he looks at me even when he thinks I'm not watching. I've felt the heat of his touch. I've felt the passion in his anger. There are so many levels that make him who he is and every one of them is special. He makes me feel special and I want to spend every day showing him just how much.

I'm tempted to change out of these ridiculous sweatpants and go find him but then I remember what he asked of me. Stay in my room and that makes me chicken out. Someone will come for me in the morning. I'll have to wait to find the opportunity to make him realize he missed me. I hope he misses me.

Instead, I take the first hot shower I've had in days. When I'm done, I slip into a pair of shorts and a T-shirt and crawl onto the bed. Feeling a need to fill the silence, I thumb through the pages of my favorite book, reading the passages out loud to myself to fill the aching silence. My mind isn't on the words though, it drifts to thoughts of Backdraft. He fills every thought I have lately. Staring at the ceiling, I think of how he went back to the compound, despite the danger of getting caught, just to get me my things so I wouldn't be without. That's the greatest thing about this man. Since the moment we met, he's put my needs before his own safety. I've never had anyone do something so special for me, and even if he never returns, if whatever we started is already over, the memory of that act will always be special to me.

I must have fallen asleep because I wake to the sound of the door opening. On instinct, I jump and crawl back towards the headboard drawing the covers up around me. My vision is blurry from sleep, so I scrub my fingers over my face to clear them. That's when I see Backdraft standing over me. There's a look in his eyes that I haven't seen before and a smile on his lips. It brightens the darkness of his face and looks so good on him.

"Dax?" I whisper, knowing the effect it has on him when I use his real name. My intention isn't to anger him but to elicit the need it ignites in him. A need that I crave. "I didn't think you'd come."

"I couldn't stay away." Backdraft drops down beside me. He bends down and presses our foreheads together.

"I'm glad you didn't," I whisper against his lips.

Backdraft reaches out, grazing my cheek with his thumb, and warmth shoots through me. It's crazy how much I need this man and what his touch does to me. "There's so many reasons we shouldn't do this."

It looks like it pains him to say those words. Even though they feel like a hammer to my chest, I lean up, bringing my lips close to his. "I don't care about those reasons. I want you and you wouldn't be here if you didn't want me."

He responds with a softness I don't expect. His lips press to mine and part them slightly, drawing my breath from my lungs. His kiss is soft but passionate as his tongue sweeps my mouth and tangles with mine. This kiss is different from the last, like he's letting go of everything that's keeping him from allowing himself to feel something real and those emotions are all pouring out. And that's what I want to give him. Real and passionate and safe. It's something we both need more than air itself.

"I wasn't fair to you last night. Let me make it up to you."

I pull my head back leaving some distance between us and grip his face in my hands. His facial hair is rough against my palms. "We've been through this already. I wanted you then, Backdraft, as much as I want you now."

"I'm not good at this kind of thing but even I know that's not how a woman dreams her first time would be."

"That's true but I'm not complaining. I accept you, exactly how you are."

"I want to do better, Little Lamb." A low growl reverberates from his chest. "I need to do better so I can be the man you deserve."

His hand grips the back of my head pulling me to him. His lips crash against mine, hungry and needy. His tongue swirls with mine and I moan into his mouth. He kisses me with such intensity my knees weaken. The thought of what this man can do to me sends heat pooling between my legs. If it wasn't for this bed bracing me, I'd be a puddle on the floor.

"Then make love to me, Dax." I whimper my need, thrusting my hips up into him. I can feel his hardness pressed against me and it makes me feel more alive than I've ever felt before.

His mouth moves along my neck and a wave of heat washes over me, starting from my throbbing clit and spreading to every inch of my body. My nipples harden in response, begging for his touch. My fingers clutch onto his cut, and I pull him into me, not able to get close enough.

"I don't know how, Little Lamb. You make me lose control." His hot breath tickles my skin, heightening all of my senses. His teeth gently graze against my flesh as his mouth moves down my neck. I can feel the heat emanating from his body, igniting a fire within me.

"Then lose control. Just make me feel you."

His teeth sink into my skin, sending a jolt of pleasure straight to my core. Every touch, every caress from his lips, is like a fire burning inside me, building the ache and need for him to be inside me.

"Do you feel that?" He's teasing me, his hot breath on my skin taunting me with what I crave the most.

Gripping the hem of my shirt, he rips it up over my head, exposing my breasts to him. I watch him intently taking me in as he tosses it to the floor. A smile spreads across his lips before he leans in and takes one into his warm mouth and the other in the palm of his hand. He squeezes and bites at my hard nipples.

My breath comes out rushed and frantic. "More, Dax. I need more."

He pulls back, watching me squirm against the mattress. I'm aching so bad for his touch, that I can hardly contain myself. I'm a whole new woman under his thumb. While his touch is possessive and rough, I'm in control for the first time in my life. And that feeling is powerful and exciting, making me even wetter for him.

His hand slides down my stomach and trails along the seams of the cotton shorts I'm wearing. The way his rough fingers graze my skin sends a shiver up my spine. He grabs hold of them with both hands and slides them around my ass and over my ankles, tossing them to the side with my shirt. His hands glide up my thighs, the subtle brush of his fingertips against my skin leaving a trail of heat in their wake. My heart races with every inch of skin he caresses. Every nerve in my body tingles with desire, begging for more of his touch.

When his hands reach my panties, he yanks them off in one quick tug. "I like you better without these."

My heart is heaving in my chest. He grabs my knees and yanks me down the bed, his head sliding between my thighs.

The second his tongue flicks my clit, I let out a moan of pleasure. He swirls his tongue around my sensitive bud, making my body shiver. I've never experienced anything so pleasurable before and it only takes a minute for my body to shudder with the tension. He slides a finger deep inside, sending another wave of pleasure through me. My hands clench the sheets, my head snapping back with the sensation rolling through me. I whimper breathlessly as my muscles tighten, my body arching off the bed. I come so hard that my body shakes as I sink back into the mattress. He plants a kiss on my inner thigh and pulls back with a smile on his lips.

I can barely think straight as I watch him stand at the foot of the bed. I don't take my eyes off of him as he removes his cut and shirt. I roam my eyes over his chest and the tattoos and scars that cover it. His tanned skin glistens with sweat. My tongue darts to my lips, hungry to know what he tastes like. I prop myself up on my elbows and watch as he removes his jeans and boxer briefs. He leans over, gripping his hard, thick cock in his hand and flattening me back against the bed with his other hand.

Lowering himself over me, he moves between my legs and lines himself up with my entrance. I'm already quivering when he slides in slowly, pressing his weight against me. The pressure builds so intensely that I let out a long, drawn out moan as he pushes in as deep as he can. His chest rumbles as he groans his own pleasure, and it only intensifies my own knowing I'm the reason.

He props himself up on his elbows and pulls back. His thickness slides out of my pulsing heat and then thrusts back into me ripping another moan as the air escapes my lungs. I circle my arms around him, digging my fingers into his muscular back. He thrusts into me again and I arch my back, pulling him closer.

"You feel so fucking good." His deep voice shakes as he picks up the tempo. Moving in and out with hard, deep thrusts that hit all the right spots.

He's so deep inside of me that I feel him everywhere. My nerves are on fire, my body quaking around him that I can only reply with a raspy, "Mmm."

His mouth covers my lips, his tongue twirling and twisting around mine in a heated rush as he rocks into me. I roll my hips up into him, his thrusts stealing my breath as the urgency between us intensifies. My climax hits me hard. Lights dance behind my eyes and I squeeze them shut as my body throbs around him. He thrusts into me again and again as my entire body shudders under him.

Then he groans the deepest guttural sound I've ever heard and pulls out of me. One hand holds him up while the other closes around his cock. I reach up, gripping him tightly. I don't know what I'm doing but I know I want to be the one to make him come. He grips my hand with his own and works it up and down his shaft. With another deep groan, he pulses in my hand. The feeling is powerful and sexy as hell. His head jerks back as he pumps his hot release onto my stomach.

Still reeling, I release my grip and lean back onto the mattress. My eyes are closed, enjoying the feeling still washing over my body. I can't see what he's doing but it sounds like he's walking away. I pry my eyes open and sit up on the bed. He's standing in the bathroom with a towel in his hand. He turns on the water, using his hands to test the temperature as he adjusts the knobs. When he gets it where he wants it, he wets the towel and turns off the sink. Turning back, he smiles at me, the towel hanging from his hand. He returns to the side of the bed and wipes the towel over my stomach in slow, gentle strokes, cleaning himself off of me. When he's done, he turns the towel around to the dry half and repeats the movement. Who would have thought this rough man could be so gentle?

He tosses the towel onto the floor and crawls onto the bed. The mattress dips under his weight as he lays down and pulls me into his side. I sigh into him, drawing my fingertips over his chest.

"What's on your mind, Little Lamb?"

We lay there, entwined in each other's arms, the room silent except for our heavy breathing and the question rolling around in my head since we left the cabin. I'm afraid to ask because the truth could burst the bubble we're in but I need to hear it. I need him to confirm he's the man I believe him to be, and if he's not, then I need to deal with that.

Finally, I gather the courage to say, "Tell me about your father."

Backdraft's muscles tighten, his body going stiff next to mine. With a heavy sigh, he shifts his weight to sit up and leans back against the headboard, pulling me with him. "I had a dysfunctional family. My father spent his time drinking himself into a fit of rage, and with each heavy fist, my mother disassociated a little more. Eventually, all that was left between any of us was resentment. My father resented us for ruining his life, my mother resented me for his anger, and I resented them both for all of it. The truth is, I became just like him. The hatred I had inside for both of them consumed me. The only time I felt anything but rage was when I make fires. I loved how the colors merged as the flames flickered and grew higher and brighter. My obsession started with small objects, but I didn't care for the stench of melting plastic. Over the years I sought out bigger things until I found what made me hard. At sixteen, I set fire to the neighbor's barn. That's when I realized I preferred the smell of wood, the sound of it crackling, as it burned. My mother was afraid of me. My father just wanted me gone. So they sent me to Chicago to live with my uncle. He was a firefighter and the one who taught me that anyone can light a spark but only heroes could walk among the flames. He'd take me along on fire calls, teaching me how to move about safely. Although, I'm sure his intentions were geared more towards putting out fires than starting them. After fire training, I found myself setting buildings ablaze only to be the one they called to put them out. It was intoxicating and exciting. It kept me satiated for years until the day I got the call that my father had come home after a bender and beat my mother to death." I gasp. "She had become so out of touch with reality by that point that she stopped feeling anything. I went back home expecting him to pay for what he'd done, but the local police refused to file charges. They dismissed her murder as an accident. I snapped. And one night while he slept, I lit the place up."

"He deserved it." My heart aches hearing his story.

"Maybe." He shakes his head. "All I know is I never want to feel that level of rage again."

I lean my head on his broad chest, listening to the steady thump of his heartbeat beneath my ear. The words I long to say to him rest on my lips but I hold them back. I'm not sure if he's ready to hear them yet, and I don't want to fracture the delicate bond we shared. Our relationship, if that's what you can call it, is fragile and this big, strong man just came apart in my arms. It was the most beautiful experience I ever had and I doubt if there could ever be another man to make me feel like he does.

Chapter 17
Backdraft

The sudden buzz of a text message jolts Zoey from my arms. I groggily reach for the phone, squinting at the bright screen as I read the group message from Aero informing us that we're rolling out in twenty minutes and should meet at the main door. A low growl escapes my lips as I toss back the covers and reluctantly drag myself out of bed, already missing her warm touch.

"Don't go." A sharp sting zings me. I look back to see Zoey's mischievous grin and realize she's pinched my naked ass playfully.

"You're going to cost me my patch if I don't, Little Lamb. Playtime is over. Get dressed and meet us downstairs." Even as I say the words, it feels like nothing else matters except for the electricity running between us. The heavy weight of responsibility and duty settles over me, even though I want nothing more than to stay with her.

Shimmying into my jeans, I pull them up over my hips and fasten the button. While slipping on my dusty, scuffed boots, the leather soft from years of wear, I simultaneously tug my tight shirt over my head. Finally, I slip on my cut adorned with patches and symbols that remind me who I am, the familiar weight settling comfortably onto my shoulders. Before I leave, I lean down and plant a tender kiss on Zoey's forehead. "I was never here, Little Lamb."

I don't give her time to argue, I quickly make my way out of her room. The urgency in my movements is palpable as I know it's only a matter of time before someone comes to retrieve her. Aero didn't give any instructions, so I have to assume it will be him. The last thing we need is for him to catch me here.

I make my way to the door. It creaks slightly as I quietly pull it open, grimacing at the noise it makes. Peeking my head out, I scan the hallway for any signs of movement. Satisfied no one is around, I slip through and quietly close the door behind me with a soft click as a door across the hall swings open. Surge steps out, eyeing my unexpected presence in the hall. I nod a good morning when another door opens a few feet away and Crank slinks through the narrow opening like a bull in a china shop. He looks like he got dressed in the dark. As our eyes meet, he freezes and runs his rough hands through his messy hair.

"What?" he grumbles defensively under our curious gazes.

Surge's wide eyes glint with amusement as he cocks his brow and lets out a deep, rumbling laugh. "Looks like it's the dog's turn to take the walk of shame. You filthy mutt."

Crank nonchalantly shrugs his broad shoulders while Pike stumbles through another door further down the hall, frantically hopping on one foot while trying to slide a boot onto the other. He looks up at us, bleary eyed from a night of partying, and slurs out, "Bitches be crazy in the morning."

We all erupt into laughter as one by one our fellow brothers emerge from various rooms, some still half-dressed and others sporting wild bedheads. The hallway quickly becomes crowded with our rowdy group, each one wearing a satisfied grin.

Tango slides in behind me, his palm landing on my back with a sharp slap. "Where did you sleep last night?"

Sweat beads at the nape of my neck and my hand instinctively raises to it. My mind races with memories from last night and I can only hope no one heard Zoey and I.

"Don't you want to know?" I chuckle, trying to brush off the question when heavy footsteps and a rumbling voice echo from behind us, grabbing our attention.

"No one cares about the pussy you all got last night. Time to roll out." Aero barks out orders, not giving a shit about their tales of conquest as he stops in front of Zoey's door.

With a loud bang that shakes the walls, Aero knocks on her door. She opens it with grace and poise, her eyes meeting mine for only a moment before she looks away. My heart stutters at the sight of her, but I quickly compose myself as she greets us with a soft "morning."

Aero glances from the bag slung over Zoey's shoulder narrowing in on me with a pointed glare and then back again. "Good, you're ready to go. We have a long ride ahead of us. You can ride with Backdraft. Let's go."

I quickly take the bag from Zoey's grasp and lead her toward my motorcycle, eager to escape the intensity of Aero's silent questioning. I can feel Zoey's eyes on me as we walk, but I focus on securing her belongings before mounting the bike. The leather seat is warm from the morning sun as I climb on and offer her a hand up behind me. With the twist of my wrist, I rev up the engine. The rumble fills the quiet street, sending a thrill down my spine. It's good to have my bike under me again and Zoey at my back.

I can't contain my smile when her hands grasp tightly onto my waist, her body pressing against mine. It's everything I imagined it'd be. As I pick up speed, the wind rushes past me carrying her tantalizing scent with it. Every turn brings a new rush as we deftly maneuver through the city streets leaving the bustle of Nashville behind.

***

The journey back to Atlantic City seemed endless. Zoey's arms tightly wrapped around my waist as we rode on my bike, the roar of the engine filling our ears. As dusk settled over us, we stopped for the night while Aero and the rest of the club went ahead. The countless bathroom breaks, and pit stops along the way were necessary with her on the back of the bike, but I didn't mind. Having her so close was worth every delay.

As we cruised down the open road, I could see Zoey's hair blowing in the wind and a smile lighting up her face. It was her first time riding on a motorcycle besides our dirt bike fiasco and the ride to Royal Road, which I didn't count because she wasn't riding with me. Watching her enjoy the freedom of the ride made me feel alive. I never imagined how perfect it would feel to have a woman riding behind me. Not any woman. Zoey. The way her body fits behind me is utter perfection and I wish we never had to get off this bike. I took the scenic route to extend our time together, but all good things come to an end. When I pull through the gate of our clubhouse, I come to terms with the fact that this must end too.

The loud and deep roar of the engine fills the air as I find a place to park in the crowded lot. Aero's scrappy dog barks, his tail wagging with excitement as he trots alongside the bike until we come to a stop. Turning off the engine, I keep the bike upright and sit idle for a few minutes. Zoey's arms are still wrapped around my waist, her thighs snug against my side. It's like she doesn't want this moment to end either.

A shrill whistle from the steps grabs my attention and the dog panting beside my bike takes off running toward the sound.

"Are you going to sit there all day or are you coming inside?" Surge, our club's Sergeant at Arms, snarls at me from his spot at the top of the stairs.

"What's it to you?" I growl, pissed at Surge for wrecking the moment.

"Not a damn thing but Aero's been waiting for you."

Fuck.

I wonder how much he knows about Zoey and me. I've tried my damndest to be discreet until I can come clean and tell him the truth, but I've caught his glares when he's noticed us standing too close or our hands lingering a tad too long. He's probably waiting to chew my ass out for taking my sweet time getting back. Zoey shifts on the seat behind me, the loss of contact is like a nail in the coffin. The end of us. I will be forced to let her go and the thought of that aches more than I thought it would.

"Tell him to keep his panties on. We just got here," I growl.

Surge raises his brow. "You want me to tell him that?"

Fuck me. "No."

"Then stop dicking around and get off already."

I haven't gotten off since early this morning, before Zoey and I left the motel room we shared last night. It already feels like it's been years since I've touched her and my cock aches at the thought of never getting that chance again. I don't know what is in store for us once we walk through that door, which is why I've delayed it for as long as possible. One thing is certain, if given the chance to bury myself between her legs again, I'll take it. Inside her is where I belong.

I run my hand over her leg, signaling to her we have to move. Reluctantly she swings her leg over and dismounts. I miss her warmth immediately.

I drape my arm around her shoulders and lead her toward the clubhouse, feeling reluctant about what waits for us.

"Where is he?" I ask Surge, stepping around him and leading Zoey into the clubhouse. I had hoped to have more time to get Zoey settled and show her around, but I can't keep Aero waiting any longer.

"He's waiting for both of you in Church," Surge informs me.

Well, shit. So much for time.

Zoey's wide eyes absorb it all. The brothers bellied up to the bar, laughing with Midge while she keeps them lined up with ice-cold beer. Grizzly passes in front of us, carrying what looks like a laundry basket. He's grumbling under his breath as he follows closely behind Mariana toward the back room. We exchange a glance and I recognize the look of a man desperately masking his desire with a grumpy facade before his eyes dart back to Marianna's backside. There's too much to unpack there right now so I file it away to throw in his face later.

Padre spots us and chuckles, "Hope you enjoyed your ride." Tilting his head towards Church.

Passing through the courtyard, we catch the eye of Emery and Lacey kicked back on lawn chairs, sunning themselves under the glass dome ceiling and sipping some fruity concoction in oversized glasses. Emery tilts her sunglasses and smiles at us.

Taking Zoey by the hand, I offer her comfort as we make our way to Church. Even though Aero's office is the size of a broom closet, Church is a strange place for a meeting with someone who isn't wearing a patch.

When I open the door, I have even more questions. Aero stands as we walk through the door. His eyes narrowed and a scowl plastered on his face. He's pissed but he will have to get over it. Rescuing Zoey might have been an assignment, but she's become more than that. She's the one who quiets the demons. She's mine and he'll have to learn to accept that.

Behind Aero sits a man dressed in dark jeans, sturdy boots, and a sleek black leather jacket. At first glance, he looks no different than the rest of us, but his body language sets him apart. He sits tall and confident, giving off a dangerous allure masked behind wealth. His hand rests on the knee of a stunning woman with loose brown curls coiling over her shoulders. She's wearing a sleek black pantsuit with a red blouse and matching heels. They look like a real power couple. The shifty fucker in the corner behind them, I know to be Kayden Black. He brought us this job and I can only assume he's here to collect. The pit of my stomach twists into knots.

Squaring off in defense, I keep a tight hold on Zoey's hand. Four pairs of eyes drop to where our hands are folded into each other. If he thinks my relationship with Zoey means he doesn't have to pay up, he's got another thing coming to him. I did my job and more. Zoey is safe because of me.

"What's this about?" I ask Aero. President or not, I don't appreciate being summoned like this and I don't care for the tension in the room.

"This is Cal and Brie Carracci, head of the New York Syndicate. They hired us to locate Zoey and return her to her rightful home."

Zoey's face twists in confusion. "Why would you do that? I don't know you."

"I'm going to be honest with you, Zoey. I need something from you," the man Aero called Cal Carracci states.

"I don't understand. What could you possibly need from me?" Zoey asks emphatically.

"Please have a seat and I'll explain. I've been informed that you've formed a bond with Backdraft, so if it makes you more comfortable he's welcome to stay."

Aero gives his approval, motioning towards the table in the center of the room. Zoey and I take a seat next to each other.

"Zoey, does the name Carmine Bianchi mean anything to you?"

"No. Should it?" I can hear the frustration in her tone and her hand squeezes tighter around mine.

"That doesn't surprise me, you've been sheltered from the outside world for so long. Carmine Bianchi once led the New York Syndicate, the organization Brie and I now run. He wasn't a good man. He was manipulating and ruthless. And you're not going to want to hear this, but he's your father." Cal lets out a deep breath.

Zoey blankly stares at him. I'm not sure if she's processing his words until she finally speaks, "I don't understand. Dominic Cassedy is my father."

"That's what they wanted you to believe, but it's not true. Dominic Cassedy was married to your mother, but he isn't your father. The truth is that your mother had an affair with Carmine Bianchi and got pregnant. When Dominic learned the truth, he murdered her and kidnapped you to punish the Bianchi family. Heirs are an important commodity in this life. I don't believe that Carmine ever knew about you. That's why Dominic kept you a secret all these years. We only recently found out and that's when we came looking for you. I know you have a lot of questions, and I'll answer them all but maybe it's best if we start slow. Our families have a complicated history and bad blood."

I mock him in my head. Complicated is an understatement. I've never met the man before today, but I've heard the stories. He's a legend. The Bianchi's and the Carracci's fought for control of the Syndicate for decades and only one man was left standing. Cal Carracci rules it all thanks to his birthright and marriage to Brie, a true Mafia Royal and legend herself. Together, they eliminated everyone who stood in their way including his brother.

"We're prepared to take you back to New York with us, set you up in an apartment, and provide you with the best security money can buy."

"To hell you will." I blurt out, forcing my chair out from under me. The wooden legs scrape against the floorboards before toppling over.

Aero is on his feet in seconds. "You might not like it, but you will sit the fuck down and show some respect or say your goodbyes now."

I don't back down. I know Aero is the President of this club, and if he wants my patch already, he can have it, but I'm not giving her up without a fight. We stand locked in a battle of wills staring each other down. I knew she was important to the people who hired us. I read the file. I read the details of her mother's death, but it never mentioned being a mafia princess. A tug on my arm breaks my stare down and I glance at Zoey and the big fat tears in her eyes. My stomach swirls seeing her pain.

"Please, Backdraft, I need you here with me." Her soft voice wraps around my heart. I pick up the chair and return to her side. "I'm willing to hear you out, Mr. Carricci, but unless Aero tells me I can't stay or Backdraft doesn't want me here, I don't plan on leaving."

"You and I will talk about this later." Aero lets his position be known but doesn't immediately deny her request.

When Aero sits back down, Cal nods his head and continues. "We hired the Royal Bastards for the recovery mission because of their extensive backgrounds and to keep the news of your existence from falling into the wrong hands. The world thinks the Bianchi bloodline is dead and it's safer if they continue to think that."

"Then it sounds like I'm safer here," Zoey states.

A subtle nod of Cal's head confirms she's right. "We could have left well enough alone, but there's no honor in that. I know what it's like to have your heritage kept from you. You deserved to know the truth. It's up to you what you do with it. We didn't bring you back to force you into a life you don't want. You've had enough of that."

"Where is this man you claim is my father? Why did you come looking for me instead of him?"

"Zoey, he's dead."

"Dead? That's convenient, the only people who can confirm what you're saying are all dead."

"Not all of them. We have reason to believe that Dominic is planning an attack on the New York Syndicate correlating with your twenty-first birthday. Aero informed me that while most of his crew have been eliminated, he got away. An attack of this magnitude will set the syndicate back by a decade. He'll need you because of your bloodline. He'll use it to take back control once we're eliminated. It wasn't the initial plan but now that we know he's still out there we need you to lure him out of hiding and end his crusade."

"Are you fucking kidding?" Aero slams his fist down at my outburst but I'm too angry to care. "You sent me to rescue her and now you want to put her in danger?"

"We have a well-trained team that will keep her safe. He'll never get close enough to hurt her." Kayden Black, a mercenary turned Consigliere to the Carracci family, speaks from his spot in the corner of the room. His voice, unlike ours, is steady and emotionless. Though he stands in plain sight, he seamlessly blends into the background, unnoticed until he chooses otherwise.

I cock my brow, not believing what I'm hearing. "Then why didn't you go get her yourself?"

Kayden takes my challenge and raises me. "Our presence would have tipped him off that we knew the truth. Using you made it look like a kidnapping and kept her out of danger."

"A lot of good that did. They almost blew her up, and when that failed, they shot at her. They were willing to kill her at the first sign of trouble. What makes you think they won't do it again?"

"Enough." Aero's face is scrunched, tight lines tugging at his forehead, "This is not our fight."

"It sure the fuck is. Zoey is mine and I won't stand by and let them play with her life."

Aero's hard eyes glare at me. "Are you claiming her?"

Ignoring everyone else in the room, I look at Zoey. Placing my hand on her arm, my eyes meet hers and that familiar spark passes between us. I don't hesitate another second. "Yes."

Aero leans back in his seat, folding his arms over his chest. "Then it appears we have a problem."

The silence that fills the room is deafening.

"Looks that way." Cal's patience is waning. You can tell he's a man used to getting what he wants but my Little Lamb isn't as docile as she looks.

"Let's take a moment, shall we." Cal's wife, Brie, places her hand on his knee. His hard expression softens, and his posture relaxes as if she holds some magical persuasion over him. It's a power I'm coming to understand. Zoey's presence soothes the inferno blazing within me. "Zoey, no one is going to force you to do anything. From here on out, you are free to make your own decisions, but we'd appreciate it if you'd consider our request. The survival of my family, my children are at stake."

Chapter 18
Zoey

I feel like I'm in the middle of some kind of twisted power struggle and I have no idea what to do. On one side, there's Backdraft, an intense, possessive man I desperately want, claiming me as his own. And on the other, a powerful woman is requesting my help.

I look at Brie and take in her appearance. She's dressed in a sharp suit, her auburn hair loosely coiling around her shoulders. She exudes confidence and authority. But underneath all that, I catch a glimpse of the sadness that clouds her beautiful eyes as she clutches Cal's hand.

I look at Cal and see something I didn't notice before. Worry. It's hidden behind his hard exterior but it's there in the lines tugging at the edge of his eyes. I wonder what kind of life he must have lived to make him so guarded.

And then there's this guy, Kayden I think they called him, standing silently but with a dangerous aura around him. He hasn't said anything since Backdraft made his claim on me and I can feel his intense gaze on me.

My heart races as I realize the gravity of the situation. These people are not just any ordinary people, they're part of something bigger, something dangerous. My head is spinning with all this new information. It all seems so surreal. The tension in the air is palpable. Everyone seems on edge, as if they're all waiting for me to make a decision. I take a deep breath and try to calm my racing thoughts.

"I'll hear you out but I don't know how I can help. I don't know how to find my father… I mean, Dominic, even if I wanted to," I stammer out finally, breaking the tense silence in the room.

Brie squeezes Cal's hand tighter before speaking again. "Thank you."

I look over at Backdraft for a moment before turning my attention back to Brie. "What do you need me to do?"

A sense of tension fills the air as she takes a deep breath, steeling herself for what she's about to say. "We need you visible," she finally answers, her voice steady but laced with urgency. "He'll be watching you and seeing you embrace your new life will piss him off. He'll reach out to you."

Backdraft interjects, his voice dropping to a low and possessive growl. "I won't let you take her away."

Brie's eyes hold a glimmer of sympathy as she turns toward Backdraft. "We have no intention of taking her away permanently. We just need her help for a few days. I promise she's free to return here, if that's what she wants."

Backdraft's jaw visibly tightens but he remains silent.

His piercing gaze meets mine and I can see the worry and fear in his eyes. A rush of emotions floods through me. It pains me to leave him behind for even a second, but I need to do this. Not just for them, but for myself. I need to figure out who I am before I can fully commit to being his. When Backdraft's hand rests on my knee, goosebumps prickle across my body. I have every intention of returning to him.

Brie interrupts my thoughts and takes my hand. "We know this is a lot to absorb, but I promise you, we will make it worth it for you."

I try to mask the frustration in my voice, not wanting to sound ungrateful. "I don't need anything from you but answers. I still have so many questions."

Brie nods understandingly. "We'll do our best to answer what we can. One of us will be with you the entire time."

"I will be too." Backdraft interjects, his eyes narrowing on them defensively.

"That's not a good idea. Your presence might scare him off."

I look between Brie and Backdraft, unsure of what to do. Part of me wants Backdraft by my side, but I also understand Brie's point. I take a deep breath and make a decision.

"I think it would be best if you stay here, Backdraft," I say, looking at him apologetically.

Backdraft's expression hardens and he grunts loudly but he offers me a nod of understanding, even if he hates the idea. "When you get back, we're celebrating your birthday and making sure everyone knows that you're officially my Ol' Lady."

The term Ol' Lady is a little offsetting, but if it means we can be together without hiding, he can call me anything he wants. A smile beams across my face. "I'll be back as soon as I can."

Brie gives me a grateful smile and takes my hand again. "Let's get started then."

"Hold on." My eyes narrow with suspicion as Backdraft strides out of the room. He returns after a few minutes, clutching a cell phone in his hand. "I programmed my number. It's Midge's phone so ignore anyone but me and promise you'll call if you need me."

"I will. I promise."

Backdraft leans in, his lips meeting mine in a deep and passionate kiss. At that moment, everyone else in the room fades into the background. His lips are warm and urgent against mine, leaving me breathless and dizzy when he finally pulls away.

Chapter 19
Backdraft

The next few hours blur by in a haze of drinking and distraction. Yet, despite the carefree indulgence of the club, a small voice inside me still can't believe Zoey left with Cal and Brie. She's out there getting a taste of their fancy high-society life. The rational part of my brain knows she deserves to explore her options and see what else is out there beyond the club. Then there's the darker side. The primal, possessive side I can't control. That part of me is going crazy with the thought of her slipping away into a world that I can't follow. A world where I don't belong.

My heart is thrashing and clawing against my ribcage at the thought of Zoey. I've never felt this way about a woman before. She's gotten under my skin and seeped into my veins. The thought of losing her sends me reeling, a primal scream building in my chest as I imagine a world without her. She's mine, damn it. I claimed her. We belong together.

Aero stops next to me, his tall frame casting a shadow over me as he leans in next to my seat at the bar. His steel-blue eyes bore into mine, cutting through the facade I've put up. "You good, brother?"

I meet his gaze, feeling vulnerable under his intense scrutiny. He knows I'm falling apart. "I'm good, Prez." I quickly conceal it, forcing a smile that feels like a lie. "Just got a lot on my mind, that's all."

He studies me for a moment longer, then with a slow nod, he breaks eye contact. "Alright then. Time for Church."

"Right behind you." I know I need to get my head in the game. Our club comes first. Our chapter is still new so there's a lot to be done to secure our position in this town and make sure we prosper. I can't allow myself to be distracted by this situation with Zoey. I swallow back the rest of my beer, wiping the foam from my mouth with the back of my hand and follow his lead. I have no choice but to trust that Cal and his men will protect her, even though I have no confidence in anyone but myself when it comes to her safety.

By the time I breach the door to Church, the rest of the club is already gathered inside. The thick scent of leather and cigarettes hang in the air. Their loud voices and laughter reverberates off the stone walls. Grizzly winces, clutching his side where the bandages cover his bullet wounds.

"Take it easy on me, boys," he chuckles. "I'm still healing up over here."

"Alright, alright, settle down. Let's get down to business." Aero's commanding voice booms over the rowdy chatter of the crowded room as he stands at the head of the long wooden table. The flickering neon Royal Bastards MC logo on the wall casts an eerie red glow over his face. His commanding eyes scan the faces before him, taking in each member of the Royal Bastards MC, Atlantic City Chapter, and the room falls silent. His eyes shift to Grizzly who sits across from him at the opposite end of the table. "First off, it's damn good to have you back, Griz. Those bullets didn't stop you for long."

Grizzly nods with a proud grin, his broad shoulders straightening up in his seat. "Takes more than a few holes to keep me down."

Grizzly, our club's VP, is the only patched member that didn't come to Nashville after me. Aero grounded him after he took a bullet a few weeks ago while helping Surge and Emery extract their revenge on the man that hurt her. He needed time to heal. It's understandable but I realize he's the only one who doesn't know about Zoey. While my claim to her has been kept between Aero and I so far, there's no way the others haven't noticed there was something going on. I haven't spoken to any of them since she left and assume they've all forgotten about her already. Something I can't seem to do, even for a minute.

"Glad to hear it. Now listen up," Aero leans forward, elbows on the table and his hands folded together. "I've been thinking that it's high time we got into some legit business. Expand our reach, bring in steadier cash flow. Royal Road in Nashville gave me an idea."

Curiosity piques around the room as the brothers exchange knowing glances. Low whistles and hoots and hollers fill the air as they start recalling their night of debauchery at Royal Road. Aero's voice rises above the noise, his eyes sparkling with mischief as he speaks, "Picture this, a one-stop vice den. Casino, nightclub, bar, the works. But here's the kicker. We'll have an underground fighting ring too, for the high-stakes gamblers and adrenaline junkies."

"I like it," Grizzly nods, stroking his thick, red beard thoughtfully. "Let us cater to all types. The suits can rub elbows upstairs while the real money moves down below."

"Exactly," Aero points at him. "It'll be classy as hell topside, bring in the big fish. Then we bleed 'em dry in the ring once they're hooked."

Murmurs of approval ripple through the club. Padre rubs his hands together eagerly. "I can already smell the money. When do we start?"

Aero holds up a hand. "I'd like to get moving as soon as possible but we gotta cover the basics first. Hashtag, I need you digging up prime real estate. Somewhere with space and privacy for the underground stuff. Crank, tap your contacts, see about equipment for the casino. Tango and Surge, you're on security detail. We need this place locked up tight."

The brothers nod, mentally shifting gears to tackle their new assignments. This is a big play for the club.

My stomach twists in knots. Stronger than the excitement is the nagging fear that coils in my gut like a venomous snake. I can't keep my mind off Zoey and all the scenarios running through my head. Is she in danger? Does Dominic Cassedy know where she is? Worse than the plaguing thoughts are the whispers of doubt creeping in. Can I make her happy? Can I give her the life she deserves? I'm a scarred, rough-around-the-edges biker. Zoey's so vibrant and full of potential. Maybe... Maybe letting her go is the right thing to do, even if it rips my fucking heart out.

I shake off the intrusive thoughts, trying to refocus on Aero as he lays out more plans. One thing at a time. The club needs me sharp and ready for whatever's coming next. I'll just have to trust that my Little Lamb will return to the fold and make me whole. Right now, I've got business to take care of.

"...the money situation," Rancor's gruff voice penetrates my spiraling thoughts. I drag my attention back to the here and now. "We ain't got the capital for a venture this big."

Pike's lips curl into a snide smirk as he speaks, his thick eyebrows furrowing above his questioning eyes. "What about the fat insurance payout Emery's getting for The Playhouse burning down? That's gotta be a hefty chunk of change."

"No way," Surge shakes his head, protective of his Ol' Lady. "You know she wants to put that towards opening a women's shelter. Help other women who've been through the shit she has."

"Emery's money is her own," Aero says firmly. "The club supports her plans, but we ain't touching those funds. It's all good though, boys." His mouth kicks up in a grin. "We've had an unexpected windfall. Carracci paid up big time for Backdraft rescuing Zoey and returning her safely. Guess the big city alpha keeps his word after all, even if he doesn't like how things played out."

Surprise ripples through the group, along with hearty chuckles and back slaps aimed my way. I accept the accolades vacantly, my mind still reeling. Cal paid the club for my service, even after I claimed her for my own. What does that mean? Is it his way of acknowledging my place in her life? Easing the way for her to stay here with me? I don't fucking know. And I hate not knowing almost as much as I hate that Zoey isn't by my side where I can protect her. Touch her. Breathe her in. The uncertainty is eating me alive.

"...matter, cause we're flush now," Aero is saying as I tune back in again. "Time to get to work, boys. Plans won't make themselves."

Hashtag looks up from his laptop screen and raises a hand. "Ah, about that Prez... Been doing some digging' and most of us ain't gonna qualify for those permits on account of our, shall we say, colorful pasts." He flashes a wry grin.

Aero nods. "I figured as much. No worries, we'll find a way. Always do."

"Even you, Pres?" Tango asks, reminding us that even though we've bonded quickly, there's still a lot we don't know about each other.

A shadow crosses Aero's face and he shakes his head. "Yeah, brother. I did a stint in the cage years back. Ain't no way in hell they'll approve me either."

Shock ripples through the club. Glancing around, it seems like I'm the only one not surprised by his confession. Every one of us ended up in this life walking the line between right and wrong for a reason. Some of us strayed to the wrong side for a while too long.

"Well shit," Rancor mumbles. "Now what?"

Aero leans forward, elbows on the table. "We get creative, is what. Hashtag, see what ideas you can come up with. In the meantime, I'll put out feelers. See if anyone in town owes us enough to let us use their name on the paperwork." Aero stands from his seat at the end of the table, "It should go without saying, I expect all of you to help Emery with whatever she needs for the shelter. We'll reconvene in a couple of weeks. Tonight, let's celebrate Grizzly healing and Backdraft returning in one fucking piece."

Chairs scrape back as my brothers disperse, heading for the bar, the pool tables, and their women. Usually, I'd be right there with them, ready to cut loose. But tonight, I'm not celebrating surviving that blast because all I can think about is a blonde-haired beauty with fire in her eyes and my brand on her skin that's not where she belongs.

Rubbing a hand over the ache in my chest, I wander out to the back deck. The muted thump of music pulses against my back as I stare off at the casino lights in the distance.

"Where are you, Little Lamb?" I murmur into the night. "I'm going insane without you."

But the only reply is the crash of the waves. I take a moment to collect my thoughts. I need to focus on the task at hand, for Zoey, for the club. I'll see her soon enough, and when I do, I'll show her that this life, our life, is where she belongs.

With a heavy sigh, I turn and head back inside to join the others. Tonight we party but tomorrow we start planning our biggest score yet. One that'll not only bring us the legitimacy we need, but also show Zoey that our world can be her world too.

Chapter 20
Zoey

I step out of the clubhouse and into the fresh, breezy air. My nerves are on fire and my heart aches having to leave Backdraft behind, even if it's only temporary. Kayden and Cal flank me like my own personal bodyguards. The breeze from the ocean caresses my face, carrying with it the scent of salt and sand. I breathe it in, inhaling a deep calming breath.

Brie smiles at me, "Are you ready?"

I nod, my stomach filled with butterflies. I can't believe I'm actually doing this. We climb into a sleek black SUV waiting for us at the curb and we're off. The engine purrs to life, vibrating underneath us as we speed through the busy streets of Atlantic City.

The drive doesn't take long, and before I know it, we pull up in front of a trendy-looking clothing boutique. Brie hops out first, her heels clacking against the pavement as she strides to the door. She's like a force of nature, bending the world to her will. A moment later, the glass doors slide open and she waves us inside.

The store is dimly lit, soft music playing in the background. Racks upon racks of clothes in every color imaginable greet me and my breath catches in my throat. I've only ever dreamed of stepping foot in a place like this, let alone trying on the expensive merchandise.

"Go ahead," Brie says, gesturing to the racks. "Pick whatever you'd like. The more, the better."

I hesitate for a moment, unsure of where to even start. I reach for a royal blue gown that shimmers in the low light, the fabric soft as silk against my fingertips. It's a size too small, but I can't help but fantasize about wearing it, strutting into a room filled with important people.

Brie chuckles, as if reading my mind. "You'll fit into it, trust me. Besides, it's your night to shine, Zoey. Time to see what you've been missing."

Her words spur me on and I begin to browse, sliding hanger after hanger past my fingertips. I've never felt so alive, so free. I hadn't realized how much I've been craving this. To live my life on my terms, not my father's or the man I thought was my father. The realization that my whole life was a lie weighs on me but I refuse to let it ruin this moment for me. I might never get a chance like this again. I don't know a lot about Backdraft, but I can tell he doesn't have the wealth that Brie and Cal have. I don't need it anyway. The memories I'm making now will last me a lifetime.

An hour later, my arms are laden with dresses in all shapes and colors, each more extravagant than the last. Cal looks amused as he holds the fitting room door open for me, but he doesn't say a word as I slip inside.

Inside the changing room, I hang each dress carefully, surveying my choices. I settle on a deep red number, the fabric draping seductively from the hanger. I slide into the figure-hugging gown, the fabric caressing my curves in all the right places. I adjust the straps, and step in front of the mirror.

The girl staring back at me is unrecognizable. Her eyes blaze with determination, and her lips curl into a triumphant smile. I look like her, the girl from my dreams, the one who isn't afraid to take what she wants.

"Well?" Brie calls out from the other side of the door.

"I'm coming!" I reply, slipping into the exquisite heels she'd picked out for me.

They're pinchy, but I'd suffer any amount of pain if it meant feeling this powerful.

The look on Brie and Cal's faces as I emerge from the fitting room is everything. Their jaws almost hit the floor and I feel a swell of pride. I feel like a modern-day Cinderella, swept away in this glamorous world of designer labels and endless luxury. But no matter how hard I try, I can't shake the feeling this isn't my fairytale. My heart aches for the leather and grease stains on Backdraft's blue jeans. The dirt caked to the soles of his boots.

"You're breathtaking," Cal finally manages, and even though I know it's part of the act, I can't help but blush.

Brie hands me a glass of champagne and I take a sip, savoring the cool, bubbly liquid as it slides down my parched throat.

"You were born to be a part of this world," she says, winking at me. I can't help but grin in response.

"Thank you, Brie," I manage to say, forcing a smile. "But, can I ask you something? Tell me more about my... My real father."

Brie hesitates, her expression turning serious. She pours us both another glass of champagne before settling in a plush chair. "Carmine Bianchi was... complicated," she begins, her voice heavy with memories. "He was a man of power and influence, but he ruled with an iron fist."

I listen intently, sipping the bubbly elixir, desperately trying to reconcile the man Brie described as someone my mother would be with. "How did you meet Cal?"

Brie's eyes soften at the mention of her husband's name. "It's a long story, but in short, we knew each other a lifetime ago. I thought he was dead and submitted to a life I didn't want. Too heartbroken to fight. When I learned the truth, that Cal was alive, I left that life behind. Carmine never forgave me for that. He kidnapped me to force me to marry his son, Angelo, again. Cal rescued me and we've been together ever since."

"Wow, that's...intense," I mutter, my mind reeling. "I can't even imagine what it must have been like for you."

Brie shrugs, as if it's a distant memory now, "What's done is done. But I see so much of Cal in Backdraft, you know."

My heart skips a beat at the mention of his name. "You do?"

"Yes, Zoey. You two are kindred spirits, bound by something special. Something others wouldn't understand. I know you feel out of place here, but I see the way you light up when you talk about him. Don't you ever doubt that you belong together."

Her words fill me with both hope and despair. On one hand, it's comforting to know that she's giving me her blessing for a future with Backdraft. On the other hand, it only makes me miss him more.

"Now come on. There's more." Brie drags me out onto the street, the sun blinding me.

Cal takes the bags from my arms, kisses Brie on the forehead and whispers in her ear. She has such a tight hold on my arm that I can't help but hear, even in his hushed tone, "You're enjoying this too much, Princess."

She swats his arm playfully, "Hush. I always wanted a sister."

When Cal leaves to place the bags in the SUV, Brie steers me down the block and into a salon.

The stylist artfully curls my hair into soft waves that cascade down my shoulders and does my makeup in an understated yet glamorous style. I barely recognize the woman staring back at me in the mirror.

"You look stunning," Brie gushes, slipping her arm around my waist. "Ready to cause a stir?"

I gulp, wondering how I let myself get talked into this again. But as we step out of the building through a different door than we entered and onto the bustling boardwalk, my unease dissipates, replaced by awe.

The carnival-like atmosphere is intoxicating, from the flashing neon lights to the cheerful music spilling out of every casino. I find myself being ushered towards one of the ritziest establishments on the strip, with Cal and Brie behaving as if they own the place. And judging by the way people part like the Red Sea for them, maybe they do.

Whispers and stares follow in our wake, but I hold my head high, determined not to let my insecurities get to me. A bevy of photographers swarm us the moment we step foot inside, their cameras clicking in a blur of flashes.

"Look this way, Zoey!"

"How does it feel to be back with your family?"

Confusion grips around me. Earlier, I was told how dangerous it was for the world to find out about me, but now, they're leaking the story to the press. I don't understand the plan and now I'm even more worried. What if it's not just Domonic we lure with this charade? What if it brings real danger with it?

Cal shoos them away with practiced ease, guiding us toward a private table overlooking the dance floor. The place reeks of money and excess, everything screaming wealth and extravagance.

As I soak in my surroundings, sipping on a fruity cocktail that packs a punch, my thoughts drift back to Backdraft. I can picture him now, lounging in his faded jeans, nursing a beer. My heart aches with longing, and I have to blink back the tears that threaten to spill.

"Hey, none of that," Brie says, squeezing my hand. "We'll have you back with your biker stud in no time."

I muster a shaky smile, hating how easily she can read my emotions. "I just... I don't know if I can do this. What if Dominic..."

"Shh," Cal soothes, patting my back. "We've got you covered. Besides, Zoey, you deserve to experience life outside of that compound. You're meant for more than hiding. Enjoy it."

He's right but the fear still sits heavy in the pit of my stomach. Tonight, I'll allow myself to enjoy this once in a lifetime experience. Tomorrow, we'll deal with the fallout.

As the night progresses, I try to push away my fears and focus on the here and now. The music is electric, the people vibrant and alive. I even dance with Cal and Brie, laughing as we twirl across the dance floor, my gown swirling around my ankles. I'm acutely aware of the eyes on us and I remind myself that they're supposed to be.

The evening continues in a blur of small talk and false laughter. I'm on autopilot, desperately trying to remember my lines, my true identity, and my mission: to lure Dominic out of hiding.

Finally, exhausted, we return to our table, where a plate of food awaits me. I pick at it absentmindedly, my gaze drifting to the door, searching for any signs of Domonic.

"It's going well," Cal says, his voice low so as not to be overheard. "He'll show himself. I promise."

But I can't shake the feeling that if this takes too long, I might lose myself in the glitz and glamor. That the old Zoey, the one who didn't care about designer labels or attention, would be gone forever. And as I look at Cal and Brie, I wonder if the risk is worth it, if exposing Dominic erases the girl I once was.

The night flies by in a blur of lights and endless champagne. It's only when the crowds start to dwindle that Cal decides it's time to call it a night.

"Come on, Cinderella," Brie teases, nudging me with her elbow.

I giggle, clinging to their arms as they guide me out of the club, feeling more alive than I have in years.

As we make our way down the boardwalk, I pray this night will sustain me through whatever comes next. Because deep down, I know that once Dominic finds me, my fairytale will end and possibly my life.

We reach the high-rise hotel and I suddenly find myself reluctant to go in. I don't want this night to end. I don't want to be alone.

"You okay, Zoey?" Brie asks.

I force a smile on my face. "Yeah, I'm just... I don't know, I'm just sorry the plan didn't work. Dominic didn't show."

"Hey, it's only been a few hours," Cal says. "There's always tomorrow."

"Yeah," Brie adds. "Now, get some rest. We've got a big day tomorrow."

As they head off to their suite across the hall, I unlock my door and step inside, locking the deadbolt behind me.

I pour myself a glass of water and sit down on the edge of the bed, running my fingers along the lace-trimmed nightgown Brie had insisted on buying. It was brought to the room for me, just like all the other clothes.

"You're going to kill him in that," she'd said, winking. I blush at the thought and quickly change out of the gown replacing it with the silky fabric.

Spotting the clothes I was wearing when I left the clubhouse folded neatly on the dresser, I reach into the pants pocket and pull out the cell phone Backdraft gave me. He made sure to disable the lock screen and remove the passcode so it's easy to find the contacts list and locate Backdraft's name. It doesn't ring long before Backdraft's gravelly voice answers, sending waves of heat straight to my core.

"Little Lamb, you okay?"

"I'm fine." I run my fingertips over the silky fabric, wishing he was here. "I'm just missing you."

"I miss you too." The ache in his voice is more than I expected but it's nice to know he's starting to let his guard down with me. "Tell me what you're wearing."

I blush at the quick turn of the conversation, but I play along. I draw the covers back and describe the nightgown I'm wearing. He growls and I can hear his breaths getting short and raspy. The room heats up as our conversation takes a steamy turn. I tell him the way it feels against my skin and he whispers the naughty things he wants to do to me. His words make my toes curl.

"I wish you were here," I whisper, my body aching for his touch.

"I'm already on my way, Little Lamb."

"You know where I am?" The butterflies in my stomach flutter. "How?"

"I've got my ways," he says, the cockiness I love seeping into his voice. "I need to feel you, Little Lamb. I'll be there soon."

I'm about to protest, to tell him it's too dangerous, when the line goes dead.

"Shit," I mutter, my heart pounding in my chest.

I bolt out of bed, rushing to the window to see if I can spot him down below. Has he been here all along?

Even though it's late, the boardwalk is still lit up like a runway, but I don't see any sign of him. My heart is in my throat as I pace around the hotel room in anticipation of Backdraft's arrival. The silky fabric of the nightgown rustles with every step I take and I nervously smooth it out. I hope he likes it, because I feel like a princess. It just so happens my prince is a biker.

There's a faint knock at the door, and my heart drops to my stomach. My breaths come in shallow gasps as I make my way over to answer it, my legs trembling with anticipation. I unlock it with shaking hands, pulling it open to greet him.

"Dax."

But it's not Backdraft standing there. My blood runs cold, fear gripping my heart like a vice.

Chapter 21
Backdraft

With a twist of my wrist, I gun the throttle on my bike, the roaring engine propelling me towards the Boardwalk like a missile. Zoey's sultry words from our phone call are seared into my mind and igniting a raging fire within me. The street lights blur as they zip by melding with the image of her in that damn lacy nightgown clinging to her curves. Every passing mile amplifies my desire for her like the heat leaching off the asphalt beneath my tires. As I speed down the road, I can almost feel her body pressed against mine, her breath hot against my neck. I know that once I have her in my arms again, she'll never miss the glitz and glam of the life she's sampling. I'll make sure of that.

I finally arrive at the grand hotel. The marble columns tower above me as I park my bike in the nearest parking garage. With a satisfying click, I cut the engine and swing my leg over the side, eager to see Zoey. My impatience drives me forward as I storm through the luxurious lobby towards her room, my leather boots echoing against the marble floors. A sly grin creeps across my face, knowing what awaits me behind her door. I can't wait to get her naked under those silky sheets.

I raise my fist to knock, but the door swings open at my light touch and my world comes crashing down around me. Alarm bells start ringing in my head. This isn't right. I know it in my bones. I rush into the dark room, my fists clenched at my sides. As I flick on the light, I am met with an empty space. There's no sign of Zoey.

My heart pounds furiously against my chest as I spot a piece of fabric on the floor. I stoop down and pick it up, running the shred of the silky, lace nightgown I'd been fantasizing about over my fingers. A scent, not hers, fills the air, musky and foreign, and it only fuels my rage. Moving further into the room, I find her purse, phone and a single earring, but no sign of her. Panic rages through my veins like wildfire, consuming all rational thought. Zoey is gone but I'll be damned if anyone will get away with taking her from me.

I snatch my phone from my pocket and dial Aero's number. I need him, I need the club. With shaking hands, I clutch the phone. He picks up after one ring.

"Aero, it's Backdraft," my voice drops to a dangerous growl. "I'm at Zoey's hotel room and she's fucking gone. Someone took her."

"Where's Carracci?" Aero asks and my rage takes a fierce turn.

"Not protecting her." I'm all but roaring now, my fury reaching all new high, even for me.

"Shit, Backdraft, we're on our way. We'll find her, brother, I promise you that." The line goes dead, but I know he's mobilizing the club and they're on the way.

I'm left with only my seething fury as I wait for them to arrive. I storm out of the room, my heart pounding in my chest like a jackhammer. I don't care if I wake the whole damn world as I barrel down the corridor, banging on every door, screaming at the top of my lungs.

A door across the hall swings open, and Cal appears in the doorway, his pants unbuttoned and his hair a mess.

"Backdraft, what the hell's going on?" Cal growls, passing the gun in his hand behind him to Brie.

"Where the fuck were you?" I roar, my fist flying before I can think twice. The satisfying impact of his jaw against my knuckles gives me a momentary sense of relief. My breaths come in short gasps as I struggle to control the urge to strike him again. "Zoey's gone, you asshole! You were supposed to be protecting her!"

Cal retaliates, his fist colliding with my cheek, sending a sharp, searing pain through the side of my face but it's nothing compared to the agony in my chest.

"Enough! Zoey's not gonna want you tearing each other apart!" Brie screams.

I step back, panting, and wipe the blood from my split lip with the back of my hand. Cal's jaw tightens as he pushes past me, storming towards Zoey's door. He throws it open and takes in the scene for himself, his eyes ablaze with anger. "Where the fuck was the guard?"

Cal turns on his bare feet, storming across the hall to Kayden's room, rage fueling every step. He raises his fist and slams it against the door, the sound reverberating through the hallway. With no response from inside, he reaches into his back pocket and pulls out a keycard. He swipes it through the reader, and when it beeps, he steps forward and pushes his full weight against the door until it swings open. I follow behind closely. Cal's face drops when we find Kayden unconscious on the floor. Cal shakes him awake, demanding answers he doesn't have.

Kayden comes around, confusion clouding his features. "What the fuck happened?"

"Dominic outsmarted us. He's got Zoey." Cal fills him in. "And the guard at her door is gone too."

"Shit." Kayden curses under his breath, scrubbing his hand down his dreary face and stumbling to his feet.

"We don't have time to worry about him right now!" I growl, my voice hoarse. "We need to find her now!"

Kayden's fingers move rapidly as he pulls out his phone and flips open several laptops on the desk. He begins to assemble his teams remotely, his brows furrowed in concentration as each screen lights up from some other location. But my attention is drawn away by the loud commotion in the hallway, signaling that my club has arrived.

"Hashtag, get your ass in here!" I shout. We need every advantage we can get and he's the only one I trust to find her.

Hashtag rushes in understanding the urgency. His laptop is already open and balanced on his arm while the fingers on his free hand fly across the keyboard. There are multiple images on his screen. One has some kind of computer code running along it, another is flashing faces in what appears to be a sequence, but I'll be damned if I have a clue what he's doing. The rest of his screen is filled with camera feeds. He gives me a rushed nod and sinks to the floor with his legs crossed and his computer resting on his lap. His intense gaze is fixed on the screen, barely acknowledging Kayden's larger setup sprawled across the desk with similar feeds. But I'm well aware of their pissing contest as Hashtag's fingers fly over the keyboard in a blur, trying to out-hack Kayden's team. I can see the determination in his eyes. He's never lost a challenge and he's not about to start now. It makes me admire him even more, although I'm not about to admit that out loud.

"We'll find her, Backdraft," Aero assures me, patting my shoulder. "We'll find her, I promise."

I nod in response, but I'm not so sure. Not when we're up against people willing to hurt the ones they're supposed to love to get what they want. Zoey's life hangs in the balance, and I swear on everything I hold dear, I'll move heaven and earth to bring her home.

My feet pace across the floor between Hashtag and Kayden, trying to find something useful in whatever it is they're doing. My mind is racing so fast I can barely make out the voices of the rest of the club out in the hall but I trust they're working just as hard trying to figure this out. Whoever took Zoey better not have harmed her, because if they've so much as laid a finger on her, they're dead. She's mine, damn it, and I'll tear this city apart to get her back.

Minutes feel like hours as they comb through the footage, my stomach twisting into knots with every passing second. Finally, Hashtag lets out a curse and my blood runs cold.

"I found something," he shouts as he angles his screen so Aero and I can get a better look. The feed from the security cameras play out on the screen. Cal and Kayden huddle in behind us as we watch a man rap on the door. My vision blurs with rage as we watch Zoey draw open the door in that little white nightgown and a smile on her face.

Fuck. She was expecting me.

Her expression falls to one of terror. I grit my teeth, my hands clenched into fists at my side as I watch Zoey try to push the door closed and the mother fucker shouldering his way through. I double over like I've been punched in the gut, the air ripping from my lungs as the door closes behind him. I have no idea what's happening on the other side of that door.

"That's not Domonic Cassedy." I bark at Hashtag, my fists clenching at my side. "Who is that?"

The image in the corner of Hashtag's screen stops on the man's face. His details sprawling across the bottom complete with his height and weight, date of birth and address but his name has Cal cursing behind me.

"Gino Moretti. You have to be fucking kidding me."

"You know who he is?" I need answers and Cal Carracci is the only one with any.

"He worked for my brother, Angelo. He had both hands back then." Our heads snap in his direction and he shrugs. "He kidnapped Brie and my daughter. He was supposed to be dead."

"Looks fucking alive to me." I'm seeing red and still have no idea where Zoey is or what this asshole wants with her.

"There's more." Hashtag's voice grabs my focus from the thoughts running rampant in my head.

The hotel room door swings open and Zoey emerges into the hallway with this Moretti character at her back. Her hair is messy and the strap of her nightgown is torn and hanging off her shoulder.

If that son of a bitch touched her, he's going to pray for death when I get my hands on him.

She takes hesitant steps toward the elevator, her eyes locking onto the surveillance camera as if she's trying to send a message. A chill runs down my spine. Does she know that we'd be able to see this footage?

"There." I point at the camera feed. "She's saying something. What is she saying?"

Hashtag rewinds the footage, zooming in on her face, and hits play again. My eyes stare at Zoey's image on the screen, studying every detail. Zoey's lips move, forming the words that send a chill down my spine.

"Bomb… Get Out…"

Shit.

Aero rushes out of the room and seconds later the shrill wail of the fire alarm pierces my ears. Urgency sets in as chaos erupts in the halls. I hear my brothers barking orders as hotel guests fill the hallway. Kayden shields Cal and Brie as they take off toward safety. I curse under my breath. I know they're important people and it's his job to protect them, but what about Zoey? They're the reason she's even here.

"Everyone get out. Now," Aero orders from the doorway.

"We're right behind you, Pres," I reassure him.

"Don't fuck with me, Backdraft. We'll find her but we need to be alive to do that." Aero turns back to the hallway and I return my focus on Hashtag.

"Time's not on our side, Hashtag. Find her. Where did they go?"

He returns his focus to the monitor, his fingers trembling as they fly over the keys. "This doesn't make any sense."

"Talk to me, Hashtag."

Hashtag brings up another camera feed and shakes his head. "I don't get it. From what I'm seeing, they never left the hotel."

"How can that be? Where is she?"

Hashtag shakes his head, "I don't know. They never get off the elevator."

"Is there a floor without cameras?" My head is spinning with questions, "What about the roof? They had to have gone somewhere?"

A few more keystrokes and Hashtag has the hotel blueprints pulled up. "There's a service corridor off the first floor but there's no cameras."

Fucking hell. She's been right under my nose the whole time.

Hashtag closes his laptop, tucking it securely under his arm. Together, we burst out into the hall and join the stream of people rushing down the stairs towards the nearest exits. The sound of panicked footsteps echoes around us as we descend several flights of stairs. I spot Aero and the rest of our club up ahead helping guests who need assistance. Knowing my brothers are safe and almost out of the building, I slow my steps.

Hashtag notices my hesitation and turns to me. "Backdraft, what are you thinking?"

I shake my head. "I'm not leaving without her."

"You'll need a passkey to access the service corridor."

"Already got one." I hold up the key I swiped from one of the hotel staff a few floors up. "You did good, kid. Now get out of here."

The rush of people fades away as I turn back and head toward the elevator. With a press of a button, the polished metal doors slide open, and I slip inside, releasing a sigh of relief as the doors slide shut. I press the button for the main level and insert the key into the slot. Adrenaline builds in my chest as I watch the numbers tick by. She's here, somewhere in this building and I will find her.

The elevator doors open onto the opposite side and I step out into the service area, my heart racing with each step I take. She's close. I can feel it. I can feel her.

The cold concrete walls close in around me sending a chill down my spine as I walk further in. The fluorescent lighting back here is dull and yellow compared to the LED lights in the rest of the hotel. It casts flickering shadows along the floor, turning every nook into a potential hiding spot for a bomb. I step cautiously, looking for potential traps and explosives.

The blare of the fire alarm assaults my ears as it reverberates around the enclosed concrete space. I scan the barren walls until I spot the intrusive device overhead. With the tip of my knife, I dismantle the red plastic device and separate the wires until the horn silences in my hand. Its vibrations still echo in my head as I struggle to focus on my surroundings and listen for any signs of Zoey.

I follow the hum of the air conditioning units and the rhythmic rush of water moving through the pipes that run the length of the ceiling. My boots echo against the concrete floor mingling with the buzz off the endless rows of mechanical equipment. I move deeper in and find myself forced with a choice to go left or right. Both lead deeper into the massive room lined with more equipment.

I scan both paths with a growing sense of unease. I glance down the left side and then the right, repeating the motion several times. I need to find her and fast. If there is a bomb, I have no idea how long I have until it either detonates or the bomb squad moves in. I close my eyes and inhale a deep breath, letting my instincts guide me. Opening them, I turn to the left. Pushing on past more rows of equipment. The urgency in my steps grows with every passing second. Nearing the end of the hall, I freeze in my steps when I hear the soft whimper of her voice.

Chapter 22
Zoey

Justin shoves his way into my room, despite my attempt to keep him out. His cold dark glare narrows in on me, turning my skin to ice. I swallow hard, masking the fear that wants to steal my breath. I've never trusted Justin but he's the last person I expected to be standing outside my door.

"What are you doing here?"

He closes in on me as the door clicks shut behind him. My steps falter as I walk backwards on shaky legs, stumbling over my own feet but staying upright.

"Look at you all whored up for your biker rat." His hand grips around my arm. His fingers digging into my skin like claws. "Is that what you've become, Zoey? A whore?"

With a sneer, he rips at the strap of my nightgown. The thin lace tearing at the seams and falling loosely over my shoulder. His eyes drop to my exposed skin as I swing my fist but it misses its landing. Justin's hand darts up and closes around my neck.

My heart pounds against my chest, my breath coming out in ragged gasps.

"Backdraft will be here any minute and he's going to kill you for touching me."

His chest heaves with maniacal laughter. "He'll be too late."

"Too late for what?' The words scratch at my dry throat.

"There's bombs all around this hotel, and in less than an hour, they're going to blow. Unless you come with me, the death of all these people will be on you."

His warning hits me harder than any physical blow ever could. My stomach clenches in knots. All these innocent people, Cal and Brie, Backdraft... All their lives are in danger.

I can't hold back the tears that swell in the corner of my eyes. "Why? What do you want?"

"Isn't that obvious, Zoey? I want what was promised to me. I want you."

My heart sinks into the pit of my stomach. Justin has always been obsessed with me, but I never thought he'd go to such extremes.

"You don't have to do this, Justin." My voice trembles.

"I do, Zoey." His grip around my neck tightens, his eyes void of all emotions. "You've left me no choice. Now let's go."

With his hand still around my neck, he slings my body towards the door with a force

I never knew he was capable of. I take slow hesitant steps out of the hotel room and into the hallway, knowing that there's no other choice. If I scream for Cal or Kayden's attention or stall until Backdraft arrives, hundreds of innocent people will die. My only choice is to placate him and hope he doesn't detonate them anyway.

As we make our way down the hallway towards the elevator, I spot the security camera overhead. In a desperate attempt to warn someone, anyone, I carefully mouth a warning.

Stepping into the elevator, the door slowly closes around us. My hands grip the hem of my nightgown, wishing my fingers were curled around a weapon. A gun, a knife, anything to defend myself against him, but I have nothing. Justin grunts, shifting closer. His hot breath sucking the air out of the small space. His eyes sweep over my body, lingering too long on my chest and I suddenly realize how exposed I am. He didn't even give me time to change or cover up.

I cross my arms over my chest hiding the swell of my breasts the best I can. I can feel his eyes on me, watching my every move. A feeling I've become all too familiar with. Goosebumps run down my arms and I try to hide the shiver that follows.

The elevator comes to a stop but the doors don't open. Justin inserts a key and a door I didn't notice before slides open at my back.

"Where are you taking me?" I ask, desperate for answers.

"There's someone I thought you'd want to say goodbye to."

With a forceful shove, I stumble out of the elevator. My heart is lodged in my throat, thinking about who he could mean. I've never been a religious person, but I send up a silent prayer to any god who'll listen that it's not Backdraft.

Justin leads me through a maze of concrete corridors full of oversized industrial equipment. The cold air bites at my skin and I tremble from both the cold and the fear that has a hold of me. His heavy footsteps and the thudding of my heart echo around us as he leads me deeper into the massive space and only stopping when we reach the farthest point.

"Through there." Justin motions towards a door, now brandishing a gun in his hand.

Slowly, I twist the handle and push open the heavy metal door. It's dark inside, the only light casting across the floor from the corridor behind us. The weight of the door slams shut, the thud jolting through me like thunder. Justin flips on the light and my heart stops beating at the sight in front of me. My mouth opens and slams closed, my words stuck in my throat.

My father, or the man I always knew as my father, is slumped forward in a chair. His hands and legs are bound, his fingers twisted and broken.

"Why?" I manage to croak out. As much as I hate the man for what he's become and what he's made of me, a part of me doesn't want to see him hurt. "Why did you do this to him?"

I step to him but Justin's arm slides around my waist, stopping me from moving forward.

"He broke his promises." Justin's warm breath crawls over my neck. "You caused this, Zoey. His blood is on your hands. And I won't hesitate to kill you too if you betray me." Justin shoves me forward, releasing his hold on me. "Say goodbye. We have to go."

I rush to my father, kneeling before him. Despite everything, my heart is breaking seeing him like this and knowing it's because of me. "Dad?"

I touch his face being careful not to hurt him. He lifts his head revealing the bruises and blood coating his skin. His eyes are so swollen he can hardly open them when he looks at me.

"I'm sorry, Zoey." His raspy voice breaks, tears forming in his eyes.

"What did he promise you?" I ask Justin.

His dark eyes narrow. "You, Zoey. He promised me you, but then you took off, abandoning your family and ruining everything for that dirty biker."

"I don't know what you're talking about."

"Don't play dumb, Zoey. I saw you with Carricci, which means you know the truth but maybe you need to hear it from him."

Justin stalks behind him, grabbing him by the back of his head and jerking it backwards.

"Tell her, Dad." He draws out the syllables mockingly as if it disgusts him to say it. "Tell your daughter what you did."

When he doesn't speak, Justin jerks his head harder. His shallow breaths turn into a gasp before he admits what I already know in my heart to be true. "I took your mother's life."

I stumble backwards, unable to hold myself upright. "Then it's true. All of it? I'm Carmine Bianchi's daughter?"

My father's sins seep through the cracks in his facade. The crinkles on his face draw tight. Justin lets go of his head, but he doesn't say anything, only lowers his eyes to the blood splatter on the floor with a single nod.

"Where do you come into all of this?" I ask Justin.

"Your father promised that if I helped him eliminate them all, I could have you. Imagine what we could do, Zoey. A Bianchi and a Moretti. Once the Carracci's are eliminated, we'll be the next in line to run the New York Syndicate. We could've had it all. Parties, a huge house, run the world's largest mafia organization outside of Italy but you chose to fight me at every turn! Not anymore." Before I can speak Justin pulls his gun and presses the barrel against Domonic's forehead. "Say goodbye to Daddy. You're mine now."

The sharp echo of the gunshot ricochets off the walls and I draw in a shaky breath watching as Dominic crumples in front of me. At the same time, the hotel's fire alarms erupt into a deafening wail, drowning out my racing heartbeat. I don't know how I know but I feel it in every fiber of my being. Backdraft got my warning. I can only hope he finds me in time.

The alarm catches Justin off guard. His eyes narrow and his jaw clenches as he paces the room like a caged animal. He knows it too.

"He's coming for me." I bite out, my words harsh and unyielding.

Justin stalks toward me, backing me toward the wall. There's nowhere to run and I have nothing to fight with. Justin's nostrils flare and the vein in his forehead bulges as he winds up to take a swing. The weight of the gun clenched in the calloused knuckles of his hand connects with my cheekbone, sending a sharp pain through my face. My vision blurs for a split second and I see stars. My eyes sting with unshed tears as I fight to hold them back. I won't let Justin see me cry. It's time I prove that I'm stronger than he thinks I am.

"Your plan is flawed Justin. I could never love you." I taunt him. His unraveling plan is making him even more dangerous, but I need to stall long enough for Backdraft to find me.

I brace myself as Justin winds back for another blow. As his fist connects with my chin, the impact reverberates through my body. My mouth fills with a metallic tang and blood trails from my lip but I refuse to fall. I stand my ground, glaring at him defiantly. He stares at me, his lips curling into a cruel smile.

"You don't have to love me, but you will learn to respect me. I've earned that much." He turns the gun toward his body and draws it over him. "Look at me. Look what I've given for this cause. If you think I'm going to just give it all up, you're not as smart as I thought you were."

I lunge for him, my hand reaching for the gun, but even with one hand, he's quicker than I am. My hand meets nothing but air. Justin smirks at me, slipping the gun into the back of his pants and strikes his hand out. It connects with my throat as a slow devious grin twists his lips. He flings me back against the wall, controlling me with his tightening grip.

I lock eyes with him and spit the blood pooling in my mouth in his face. "I'll never stop fighting you."

Justin leans into me, his hot breath stinging my face. "You can fight all you want. It doesn't change anything."

His rough fingers squeeze tight, digging into my skin and constricting my throat. I gasp for breath and he pushes me harder into the wall, pressing his body into mine. I suck in another shallow breath and he crushes his mouth to my parted lips. I can feel the anger of his kiss seeping through every inch of me. When he pulls away, I shudder in disgust, letting the whimper fall from my trembling lips.

The heavy metal door slams open, the creaking hinges filling the room. From over Justin's shoulder, I spot Backdraft towering in the doorway, a piece of his dark hair dusting across his forehead. His broad shoulders stretch the seams of his leather cut as he fills the doorway. A rush of relief fills my aching lungs.

He takes a few steps closer, but Justin tightens his grip around my neck, stopping him. "Come any closer and I'll break her neck."

I don't doubt for a second that he could, he's stronger than I ever realized.

"Get your hand off of her before you lose that one too." Backdraft's voice is calm but there's no mistaking the underlying aggression beneath it. Backdraft inches closer, his large hand tightly curled around the grip of his gun. The coiled muscles in his arms and chest tighten. His eyes roam over my battered face and his expression twists into a raw fury. With every step, he weighs the risk of firing a shot into the back of Justin's head. If he misses, however unlikely that may be, the bullet could ricochet and hit me. "I won't warn you again."

Justin drops his hand from my neck, reaching for the gun tucked behind his back.

"No." The word tears from my throat as I lunge toward Justin but his arm shoots back sending me hurling across the room. My body slams into Dominic's lifeless body still tied to the chair. The force knocks me to the ground under the weight of his dead body. His still-warm blood fills my nostrils and seeps into my nightgown, sticking to my skin. Another gunshot echoes around me followed by a heavy thud. My heart is racing and my stomach is turning as I struggle to untangle myself from Dominic's twisted limbs.

Backdraft closes the distance between us, reaching out his hand to help me up. "Are you ok?"

I nod, still trying to process what happened and collapse into Backdraft's arms. He holds onto me tightly as we stand there catching our breaths.

"Let's get out of here." Backdraft shifts his weight, pulling me into his side. "It's over."

Needing to see for myself, I look at Justin. Blood pours from the wound in his stomach, coating his shirt and pooling around his body but his chest still rises and falls in shallow waves. His dark eyes flutter open for a brief minute, his disgusting snarl still etched on his lips.

"I die," he chokes on his words with wheezing gaps, blood spewing from his mouth as he tries to speak, "you die."

His chest heaves and a gurgle rolls up his throat escaping with a heavy rush of blood as he takes his last breath.

"Shit. The bombs."

Backdraft grips my hand in his and we rush through the door into the long corridor just as the foundation trembles under our feet. I stumble but he grabs hold of me, pulling me back to my feet.

The walls shudder violently as another explosion erupts, sending thick choking clouds of dust and debris down on top of us. The hum of the machinery is replaced by the deafening groan of the steel support beams buckling overhead. My breath rips from my lungs, fast and shallow as clouds of smoke and debris pillar through the maze of twisted metal and crumbled concrete.

"Stay low!" Backdraft shouts above the hiss of bursting pipes, moving through the smoke like it's second nature to him.

His grip tightens around my trembling hand as I struggle to keep up. My vision diminishes from the thick plumes of smoke curling around us. Loose wires and twisted metal fall from the ceiling as we weave a path through the destruction. The smoke curls and swells, robbing my lungs of oxygen. I cough, my throat raw from inhaling the acrid fumes.

Every step feels heavier, my aching body growing weak from exhaustion. Backdraft slows, turning toward the loud pounding and voices to our right when a metal hatch slams open. A rush of fresh air whooshing in along with Aero's welcomed voice and a rope ladder.

"This way," Aero shouts down. "Would have been here sooner but this place is crawling with fire rescue and police. Took Hashtag a while to find another way in. We have to move fast."

"You first, Little Lamb." Backdraft hoists me up until I can reach the rungs. The twisted strands of woven rope are rough in my palms, but I grip tight and climb out through the safety hatch.

The gentle breeze feels like a soothing balm against my heated skin. I suck in a deep breath of crisp fresh air into my lungs and roll onto my side. Backdraft wraps his arms around me, pulling me close. We lie there for a minute until our shaky breaths gradually return to normal.

"Let's get out of here before we're questioned," Aero says seriously, pulling us from the first peaceful moment we've had all night.

Backdraft helps me to my feet and slips his cut over my arms to cover my still trembling body as I look at the hotel as more of it collapses into a cloud of dust.

"Did everyone make it out?" I ask, my voice barely audible over the wailing sirens of the numerous first responders on the scene.

"Yes. Thanks to your warning," Aero adds.

"What about Brie and Cal?"

"Back at the Clubhouse waiting for you."

I nod to Aero, relief flooding over me like a tidal wave although my mind is a million miles away thinking about everything that's happened in the past few days.

With my hand tucked into Backdraft's, I follow him to his bike. Before I know it, I have a helmet strapped to my head and I'm seated behind him, my arms snaking around his waist. I slide forward, straddling his hips with my thighs. Our bodies are flush, my front pressing against his back. With a quick rev of the engine, we take off, the wind brushing against my flushed skin as we speed away from the destruction, leaving my old life, the man I believed to be my father and the man whose cold eyes will haunt me for a long time, buried under the rubble. But with Backdraft at my side, I know there's a whole new life waiting for me.

Epilogue
Zoey
1 Week Later

"You look amazing," Lacey exclaims, overwhelmingly proud of the outfit she picked for me to wear tonight. I twirl in front of the mirror. A sigh drifts over my lips although there's been a permanent smile plastered on them this past week. The glittering black tank top clings to my pale skin, its thin straps delicately resting on my shoulders. The tight black pants mold to my curves, leaving nothing to the imagination. It's a bold and daring style, drastically different from the conservative and sweet sundresses I'm used to wearing. My new life as Backdraft's Ol' Lady requires a new wardrobe and she's not wrong. I look amazing and I feel sexy as hell.

"Here, wear these with it." Mariana holds out a pair of strappy high heels with open toes.

I take a seat on the edge of the bed I share with Backdraft, remove my socks, and slip into Mariana's shoes. Admiring their elegance as I stretch my leg out straight to get a better look. They're as classy and gorgeous as she is. All of the women here are beautiful.

"You have red polish on your toes." Emery grabs my foot playfully. "You know what they say about women who paint their toes red, don't you?"

I narrow my eyes at her, "No. What?"

"They give mean blow jobs." My eyebrows shoot up into my hairline and my cheeks flush red. They all laugh. A second later laughter bubbles up from my chest and breaks past my lips. The four of us giggle uncontrollably.

I've always wanted sisters and I've always wanted friends. I've found both here. Emery, Lacey, Mariana, even Midge, and Alleycat have all been great. I've never felt more a part of something than I do here.

"Are you ready, Birthday Girl?"

A wide smile stretches across my face. I stand, smoothing the creases from my pants and straightening my shoulders. "I'm ready."

As soon as we step into the common area, Emery and Lacey lock arms with me. We stroll past Rancor, Pike, Crank, and Padre shooting pool. They lower the pool sticks in their hands and smile proudly. Tango does a double take from his stance in front of the dartboard. Even Hashtag looks up from his laptop. I feel their eyes on me but not in a sleazy way. The men here have been as wonderful as the women. They're bikers, brash and rough. Each one wearing the same leather cut and proudly displayed patches that symbolize their bond and brotherhood. The tattoos that cover their skin and the scars that mark them, tell stories of who they are. I haven't been here long enough to learn them all, but in time, I will. Despite their roughness, they've shown me nothing but respect.

Aero, the club's President, despite being the youngest of them all, sits at the center of the bar with Grizzly, his Vice President, who has a long red beard and colorful tattoos that span every bulging inch of his muscles. On one side of them is Surge, Emery's Ol' Man, and the club's Sergeant at Arms, with thick dark hair, tanned skin, and piercing blue eyes. To the far side of them is Backdraft, my Ol' Man and the club's Enforcer. The sight of him brings a smile to my face, even though he hasn't noticed me yet. Granted, I spent most of my life in isolation, but Backdraft is the sexiest man I've ever seen, in my dreams and real life. Everything about him is dark, from his bronze skin to his thick black hair and haunting gray eyes.

The four are drinking as they chat in low, gravelly voices. The scent of cigarettes and whiskey hangs in the air around them. Midge looks up at us from her place behind the bar. She flashes me a huge smile and adds, "Happy Birthday, Zoey. Someone sent you something."

She reaches under the bar and retrieves a small package, handing it to me.

"Thank you." I take the box from her, surprised that something was delivered for me.

The four men spin on the bar stools and lock eyes on the three of us.

"Happy Birthday, Zoey. I like the new look." Aero compliments me as he reaches out, snaking his arms around Lacey's waist and draws her onto his lap. He whispers something in her ear that lights her eyes. The way they link together is perfection. There's something genuine brewing between them, even though I'm told Lacey isn't his Ol' Lady.

Emery elbows Surge in the ribs and he lets out a low grunt. "Um, yeah. Looking good, kid."

Grizzly simply nods his head. His attention is lost on Mariana, who's now slipped behind the bar next to Midge. She leans forward in the skin-tight red dress she's wearing and retrieves a bottle of

Chardonnay and five long-stem glasses. She fills the glasses, casting glances back at Grizzly from under her long lashes. If I didn't know better, I'd think something was brewing there too.

Backdraft's deep growl sends a heated shiver down my arms as he shifts to where I'm standing. He pulls me into him, his hardness pressing into the curve of my ass. He leans in, whispering in my ear, "I can't wait to tear these off of you later, Little Lamb."

"Party first," I swat at his hands clenching tightly to my waist, "playtime later."

"Are you sure I can't tempt you to make this a private party?"

"You do nothing but tempt me," I purr, pressing my ass against him. The past week we've hardly come up for air and I'm loving every minute of it. In my wildest dreams, I couldn't have imagined ever finding someone as amazing as Backdraft.

Backdraft grunts a frustrated breath and I love I can stir that need in him as easily as he can me. "What's in the box?"

"I don't know." I turn the small cardboard box over in my hands and open it. Inside is another smaller box covered in shiny silver wrapping and a folded piece of paper. I unfold the note and read it. "It's from Cal and Brie. They're sorry they couldn't be here to celebrate with us. It says this is for protection and luck."

The rumble that rips from Backdraft's chest vibrates through me. He still hasn't forgiven them for letting their guard down and allowing Justin to torment me. More so, he blames Kayden, who promised he would protect me, and maybe even himself for not being there. I don't blame any of them though. We were all blindsided by Justin's attack. It's hard to fight an enemy you can't see coming. I had no idea he was Gino Moretti, living a double life to get closer to me because of my real heritage. Granted, there might be plenty of blame to go around, but what good does it do any of us? The more I learn about what Backdraft is capable of and his role in the club, the less room there is in my heart for blame because it's full of worry that someday the same thing could happen to him.

I shake off the intrusive thoughts and open the gift, lifting a delicate gold chain out of the jewelry box. Dangling from the end is a small gold twisted horn. "It's beautiful. Put it on for me, please."

Backdraft slides the chain around my neck and fumbles with the clip in the back until it's secure. I draw it through my fingertips, admiring the meaning behind it.

Although, I don't need a charm for protection when I have a man like Backdraft.

"Turn that up." Aero's booming voice grabs our attention. We turn our heads toward the television hanging on the wall. I shiver at the images flashing on the screen of the fire engulfing the collapsing hotel. The same one that almost claimed our lives.

The newscaster's voice details the extensive damage and the condemning of the hotel. They continue to talk about the hotel's owner declaring bankruptcy and the new owner's plans to rebuild and rebrand into another casino along the strip under new management. Despite Aero's attempt to hide it, his face blanches and the muscles on his arms coil when the name Ritorno Holdings is mentioned. Aero's tight fist slams against the bar top, rattling the glasses of drinks lining it.

"That name means something to you, Pres?" Grizzly asks, breaking the uneasy silence fallen over us.

"It's nothing." Aero's grip tightens on Lacey's waist as he thrusts her off his lap. He drags his hand through his unruly, dark hair and inhales a deep, heavy breath. We all exchange questioning glances as Aero reaches over the bar and pulls himself back up with a bottle of Jack in his hand. "Don't we have a birthday to celebrate?"

Mariana hands out the glasses of wine to Emery, Lacey, Midge and I and everyone else retrieves their drinks, raising them in a toast. "To Zoey's twenty-first birthday."

Aero pops the bottle of Jack open and chugs back a large swallow, forcing a smile on his face as he strides across the room. Moments later, music is blaring through the clubhouse.

Backdraft leans closer to Surge standing next to us by the bar. "Do you know what Ritorno Holdings is?"

Surge turns to him, keeping his voice low. "Never heard of them. Maybe we should have Hashtag look into it."

"Leave it alone," Grizzly orders them, "We all know that Aero is tightlipped about his business. He'll share when he's ready."

Backdraft and Surge acknowledge his order with a nod. Despite the weight Aero's reaction left on all of us, we shrug it off and celebrate.

As the hours pass, our group grows in size as more people join the club to celebrate. The clubhouse pulses with music, laughter, and noise. I'm having the best time, drinking and dancing the night away with Backdraft and my new family at my side. The air is thick with beer and cigarette smoke, but I inhale a deep breath, letting it wash over me. I may still be figuring out who I am, but I know this is where I belong.

Also by Kris Anne Dean

Royal Bastards MC
No Way Out Book 1
https://mybook.to/NoWayOutRBMC
Scorched Souls Book 2
https://mybook.to/ScorchedSoulsRBMC
Book 3 Releases 11/04/2025

Krymson Destroyers MC
Sinful Deeds Book 1
https://bit.ly/SinfulDeeds-AMZ
Sinful Lies Book 2 https://bit.ly/SinfulLies-AMZ
Sinful Need Book 3
https://mybook.to/SinfulNeedKDMC

The Vendetta Trilogy (A Mafia Romantic Suspense)
Resurrection Book 1
http://bit.ly/ResurrectionAMZ
Reign Book 2 http://bit.ly/ReignAMZ
Retribution Book 3
http://bit.ly/RetributionAMZ

Stand Alones
Taste of Sin (Global Outlaws Syndicate)
https://mybook.to/TasteofSin-GOS

Don't miss the next release!

Thank you for reading this story. I'd love to invite you to sign up for my mailing list, so you never miss out on a new release. This series will continue and there are many more projects in the works.
Sign up for my mailing list/newsletter here:
https://bit.ly/KrisAnneNewsletter

You can also connect with me on the following platforms:

Website: https://krisannedean.com
Facebook Author Page: bit.ly/FBKrisAnneDean
Facebook Reader Group:
https://bit.ly/KrisAnnesJaggedReaders
Amazon: http://bit.ly/KADAmazon
Goodreads: bit.ly/GRKrisAnneDean
BookBub: bit.ly/BBKrisAnneDean
Instagram: http://bit.ly/KADInstagram

Acknowledgements

I would like to say thank you to my readers. You make every moment I spend writing worth it. Thank you for your support.

There are so many amazing and supportive members of my circle that deserve thanks. My editor Sarah DeLong. My sister Jamie (aka J. Lynn Lombard) you have contributed so much to my journey, and I never would be able to do any of this without your support and encouragement. Elise Gedicke, I appreciate all the help and support you give me. From here on out you and Jamie will be referred to as the Bob squad… I'm glad I made you laugh. lol

Michelle, Joy, Courtnay, and Heidi, thank you for all the work you do to get my books in front of readers. Thank you to everyone on my ARC Team.

And of course, my husband and my children for suffering through my insanity and last but not least my partner in crime Jamie D, your support and encouragement mean the world to me.

I am really enjoying the way this series is turning out. Stay with me to see what these Bastards will get into next. There's a lot more to come!

About the Author

Kris Anne Dean
Romance with a Jagged Edge

"Imperfection is beauty, madness is genius and it's better to be absolutely ridiculous than absolutely boring." Marilyn Monroe -1960

Kris Anne Dean is an indie author and lover of all things alpha. She loves the bad boys and the women strong enough to stand with them. She enjoys reading books, watching TV series and movies that feature the troubled, morally challenged anti-hero with a big heart when it comes to family. Throw in a hot body and beautiful eyes and she's a fan.

Kris Anne is a mother to three boys with an age gap between the oldest and youngest of 14 years! When she's not working, reading or binge-watching Netflix, you can find her on the sidelines cheering them on.

Kris Anne grew up in South Florida but is raising her children in Lancaster County, Pennsylvania. While she enjoys the small-town life, she hates shoveling snow. She's always on the go, always running late (blame the cow crossings and horse and buggies) and often forgets to breathe!